ABSOLUTE EROTICA

By

Elizabeth Chamberlain

TRAFFORD PUBLISHING

 www.trafford.com

North America & international
toll-free: 1 888 232 4444 (USA & Canada)
phone: 250 383 6864 ♦ fax: 812 355 4082

Dedicated to all lovers, all the world over. Bless each and every one of you.

And also to Alan Bates, a truly inspiring man and a brilliantly funny playwright. He has given me many ideas and much pleasure. I offer you my special thanks.

Alan wrote the play LUST IN THE DUST that is mentioned in INDULGENT WEEKEND and is published by New Theatre Publications.

All characters and situations in this book are purely fictitious and any resemblance to situations or people living or dead is purely coincidental

The stories are pure erotic fantasies. In real life please practise safe and responsible sex.

CONTENTS

THE PASSER BY

I awoke to another boring day of my very boring life. I was fifty years old, overweight and my husband had left me. My daughter was now married and had flown the nest and I was alone with no prospects of anything of a romantic nature on the horizon. I was a part time librarian, it was a job I enjoyed, but again it was a small provincial library so there were little or no prospects there either.

I had just had a shower and with a towel wrapped around me I went into the kitchen to put on the kettle. The kitchen was at the front of the bungalow and looking out onto the road and fields beyond; I could see the Labrador man was walking past. I call him that because I don't know his real name, but at this time of day he always walked past with his dog and if he saw me in the window he would wave. I had seen him out and about for nearly thirty years and we even said hello on occasions. He was a tall, not bad looking man approximately the same age as me. He had a lovely head of greying wavy hair. His daughter was in the same class as Claire at school and occasionally I would see him with her, but I never really got to know him. I knew he lived close by, but not exactly where.

I finished breakfast and decided to leave the plates in the sink for washing later; it was time to get dressed for work. As I put them to soak the Labrador man was on his return journey. As luck had it he saw me and waved, I returned his wave and as I did so my towel fell off and the poor man was treated to the sight of my sagging breasts. At least it stopped him in his tracks and he had a good look, or maybe it was his dog sniffing at the lamp-post that stopped him. Anyway he smiled and raised his eyebrows in approval. I could feel my face turn the color of beetroot as I rapidly folded my arms over my breasts. As he pulled his dog away he waved again and like an idiot I waved back giving him another eyeful of my tits. I quickly recovered my towel, cursing myself for being such a stupid idiot and went through to the bedroom and dressed for work.

Later that day, after work, I was waiting for my bus and it started to rain, then I remembered I had left my umbrella at the library. I cursed as I realised that I was in for a soaking, and as I pulled up my collar a car stopped in front of me.

'Can I give you a lift?'

It was the Labrador man. I felt my face starting to blush again as I remembered the events of this morning. 'Oh yes, thank you,' I stammered.

I got into the car and we drove off. 'Look I'm very sorry about what happened this morning.' I said.

'Nothing to apologise for.' He said as if it happened all the time. 'In fact you have a beautiful figure.'

I was immensely flattered and felt a glow inside that I hadn't felt for many years. We pulled up outside my bungalow and I thought to myself, 'act woman before it's too late.' 'Er would you like to come in for coffee?'

'Yes, that would be nice.'

We sat on the settee and talked about our respective children and how they had progressed in the world. We exchanged our own life stories and just generally waffled on about things in general. I must admit I felt warmly comfortable in his company. He took a final sip on his coffee then put his cup on the table.

'Can I ask you something?'

'Yes.'

'What's your name?'

'It's Jayne.' I giggled, realising that after all these years that we didn't even know each others names. I only knew him as the Labrador man, I wonder if he had a pet name for me.

He offered his hand. 'I'm Peter.' He said.

We talked on about this and that and it transpired that he had been widowed for some years and never remarried. He worked as an exhibition designer from home and it was just him and his dog. He had a warm and honest personality and I felt like getting closer to this man.

We had finished our coffee and it was one of those electric moments when you know that there is chemistry at work. We looked into each others eyes and it happened. He leaned towards me, our lips met and we embraced. As we gazed again into each others eyes it felt as though we had known each other intimately for years, it felt so right, so destined, we kissed passionately and I knew it was meant to happen. I felt a warm glow inside. We had only been in each others company for barely an hour, was I doing the right thing, I thought. 'Of course you are you silly woman, how much time do you need, you've known him casually for thirty years,' I told myself. I could feel Peter's hand travelling up my side. I sighed with pleasure when it reached my breast and I knew there and then that I wanted him. It was happening so fast, even indecently fast, but I wanted it, I wanted him.

I stood up, took him by the hand and led him through to the bedroom. It had stopped raining now and the sunlight cascaded across the bed in gentle ripples as a breeze slowly waved the lace curtains. The effect was magical, as if the bed was a shrine of pleasure highlighted by a celestial force. Peter closed the door behind him and leaned against it. He stared at me. In his eyes I could see fiery passion, but I could also detect a slight nervousness. I had to admit I had slight reservations myself, after all I had not been in this situation for many years and my body was not exactly in its prime. How would it appear to Peter, how would it perform? Somehow I thought he must be thinking the same.

Oh, to fuck with it, I thought. I reached behind my neck, lifted my hair, and released the clip at the top of my dress then my arm up my back and unzipped. I slowly pulled it from my shoulders. Peter gasped in what I hoped was pleasure as I revealed my podgy shoulders and upper arms. My dress fell to the floor and I could feel myself holding my stomach in, then I thought relax, I couldn't do this for the rest of my life. I was overweight, so what.

Peter walked slowly towards me and took me in his arms and kissed me passionately and I melted into warm wondrous bliss. I could feel his hands caressing my back and ultimately finding the clasp of my bra. With very little effort he released it; I felt the tension go as he eased the straps from my shoulders. He stood back slightly as he gently pulled my bra away. I felt my breasts sag as their support was removed, wobbling gently as they fell from their cups. They were big I had to admit, but the combination of the passing years, overeating and the effects of gravity had taken their toll and they drooped. Looking down I felt slightly ashamed as they lolled over my equally large stomach. I stood there wearing only my knickers and my thigh length stockings. Peter was silent and I was feeling slightly ashamed and I folded my arms over my sagging breasts gathering them in.

Peter unbuttoned his shirt and threw it aside. With equal measure he did the same with his trousers shoes and socks until he stood there in only his shorts. I was feeling the tingles of pleasure stirring within me. His body was pleasant but not perfect, age for age it was in a similar condition to mine and I felt more his equal now. I could see the shape of his penis within his shorts and thought of its splendour and the joys I could bring to it and the pleasure it could give me. He slid his fingers down his hips into his waistband and slowly slid his shorts down. His penis hung free, and what a magnificent sight it was. It seemed quite large, I don't know what the exact dimensions were, but it seemed more than ample to me. It was at the early stages of arousal and still hung down, long and fat. His shorts reached his middle thighs and gravity took over from there and they fell to the floor and were kicked away. He put his hand on his lower abdomen and let it slowly slide down to his manhood. He took it in the palm of his hand and gently and tantalisingly slowly slid back his foreskin with his thumb and forefinger to reveal a huge bulbous purple glans. Like a giant bell with its rim standing proud from the shaft of his penis. I imagined this broad rim inside me rasping the inside of my love tunnel.

By now Peter was fully erect and he moved towards me with his now stiff ramrod, like a flagpole before him. I swallowed as I saw this huge object of pleasure coming closer. I felt my cunt tingling and becoming moist and as I shuffled from foot to foot I could feel the wetness between my lips as they slid together in eager anticipation of what they would soon receive. I felt a mixture of yearning and anticipation and with breasts still firmly gathered within my folded arms I stepped backwards, to be stopped immediately by the wall. Peter took my wrists firmly and roughly pulled my arms apart and pinned them against the wall slightly above head level. This both frightened and thrilled me. He had a sudden overwhelming power and I trembled slightly as I was at his mercy, I was his slave, pinned against a dungeon wall my breasts exposed for his pleasure. Continuing this little fantasy I lifted my face to the ceiling and cried out. 'Oh Peter, take me. At the same time still pinned to the wall I wriggled in submission letting my huge tits shake about. This seemed to inflame him to greater heights of passion and still holding me against the wall he roughly kissed me and I could feel his huge hot cock pressing against my stomach. He released my wrists which were beginning to hurt from his strong grip and he took me in his arms and kissed me with loving passion. I in turn flung my arms around him and returned his passion. All the time I could feel that throbbing cock and kept thinking of that huge ridged bell end thrusting inside me.

He took my tits as he kissed me, groping and fondling them like a being possessed. He then slid to his knees and continued to fondle me and kiss and suck them like a baby. It was wonderful. They had longed for attention for all these years. I had been ashamed of them and had even considered having them surgically corrected. As I watched Peter devouring them like a child with chocolate, it completely dispelled any notion of that possibility. He was now my slave and it made me smile at the power that my tits held over him.

As he continued to suck me I could feel his hands clutching my knickers, which were now soaking wet with my passion juice. His breathing became heavier as he kissed my belly, getting lower and lower, and then slid my knickers down my thighs to the floor. I still had on my thigh length stockings and I could feel Peter rubbing his face against the silkiness of the top. He kissed the white flesh of my thighs gradually getting higher. So slowly he went, so slowly it made my body ache. I knew where he was going and I mentally urged him on. Eventually he reached my pussy and he kissed it so sweetly. After a few seconds I pushed his head away gently and as he kneeled there longingly, I slowly walked over to the bed. I turned to face his kneeling figure and put my hands on my chest and let them slowly follow the contours of my tits. Taking one in each hand I performed for his pleasure. I pushed them together and pushed them up creating the ultimate cleavage, holding in my stomach and forcing out my chest to great effect. Peter gasped and whimpered. I let them drop and they swayed and wobbled. My hands flowed down my side to my hips and I bent forward to let my tits hang free, rotating my shoulders they swayed like majestic melons tantalising Peter to a torturous pleasure. He was spellbound by the sight and his cock was throbbing with desire. I lay down on the sun dappled bed the shafts of sunlight dancing over my body. Peter came to stand by the bed. I raised my knees and slowly opened my legs. I could feel my juice flowing and I could feel my lips opening. Peter gasped again as he stared in wonderment at my womanhood. I slid my hands slowly down my tummy and between my legs and I pulled open my lips so he had a full view of my glistening pinkness. 'Lick me.' I whispered.

Peter kneeled beside me and gently kissed each breast in turn, then kissed my tummy and slowly kissed lower and lower towards my yearning slit. The journey seemed endless but it made my desire stronger. Faster I whispered, faster. Eventually he reached my mound of Venus and he kissed my aching lips. I let out a gasp of pleasure as he reached his goal. Still kneeling beside me his arms slid round my thighs. Then he went to work on me. His tongue slid between my lips and slowly travelled down to my love tube and his tongue went inside. It was unbelievably erotic. He tantalised my hole so beautifully, then his tongue travelled up between my lips to my clitoris. It was fantastic and I let out a little scream of pleasure. Then he travelled down to my love tube again and pushed in his tongue as far as it would go. Then back to my clitoris again. This time he gave it all his attention and licked it up and down and round and round. He clutched my thighs pulling them wide open, which also served to open my lips wider giving him greater freedom to lick me. On and on he went whipping me up into a sexual frenzy. I could hear the sound of his tongue slavering over my bursting clitoris. As he knelt beside me I let my hand slide over his muscular buttocks and between his legs. I found his balls and what a pair they were. I juggled them between my fingers very gently. Then I went to work on his now enormous shaft. I let my hand travel its length until I found the bulbous end that I yearned for. I clutched his shaft and let my hand travel its whole length, backwards and forwards. It was so thick I was unable to close my fingers completely around it. As Peter continued to lick me I continued to stimulate his cock. I heard him groan with pleasure and I could feel at the end of his shaft a bead of semen was seeping out. What to do, I thought, shall I rub him faster and make him come, or go gently and save his pleasure for me. I chose the latter.

The inevitable was happening; I could feel the electricity of orgasm building up inside me. Peter detected this and concentrated harder on my clitoris, he also slowed his rhythm which made my orgasm build more slowly but more intensely. It gripped me. I was out of control, it overwhelmed my whole body. That agonising pleasure that just takes you over, leaving you to scream helplessly with the ultimate passion. It reached its peak and I just screamed out 'Peter I'm coming.' I gripped his side and my fingers dug into his flesh. I cried out loud as the orgasm seemed to go on for a frighteningly long time. Peter continued to lick me and for a moment I thought this body consuming pleasure wasn't going to stop. It was indeed ecstasy and fear combined. Eventually the orgasm started to subside and Peter continued to lick me sustaining a sort of lesser orgasm. He finished off by sucking my clitoris which was a unique pleasure in itself. 'Oh Peter, that was unbelievable,' I whimpered.

It was now his turn and he kneeled between my thighs taking hold of each of them so my feet were over his shoulders. I reached down and guided Peter's mighty cock inside me. I felt his shaft part my lips and slowly slide inside me. I had just experienced the orgasm of my life but I wanted to be fucked and fucked hard. Peter did not disappoint me. His shaft had travelled its full length and I could feel the ridge of his glans stimulate me as I imagined it would. I took his full length, but only just and as he continued to thrust with greater passion I could feel it slamming deeply inside me. As he held my thighs he lifted me off the bed so I was level with his shaft and he gave me maximum penetration. On and on he went ramming his huge cock harder and harder into my eager little cunt. He reached an orgasmic frenzy and he rammed me so hard I thought I would burst. His face contorted with the same agonising pleasure that I had enjoyed a few minutes earlier. I could feel his shaft pulsate inside me and with a mighty roar he let fly with all he had. His hot semen shot inside me in waves, I could hear it squelch and felt it oozing from me as he gave me the last few remaining thrusts.

He knelt there gasping and still holding my thighs with his shaft still inside me. The dappled sunlight still rippling like waves on our bodies.

'Oh Jayne, that was wonderful.' He sighed.

What a fantastic afternoon and what wonderful luck to meet someone like Peter. I hope this was to be the beginning of something incredible.

HUNGARIAN GOULASH

I had met Garry through an advertisement in the local paper, you know the sort of thing, "Shy male divorcee, emotionally scarred, would like to meet sincere sympathetic lady, of any age for friendship and maybe meaningful relationship." Well he said any age and I am sixty three, so I went for it. We had our first date two weeks ago, a very pleasant meal in a very nice restaurant and since then we had a number of evenings out, theatre, restaurants etc. It all seemed to be going well. The only misgiving I had, if you could call it that, was our age difference. He was thirty five, so there were nearly three decades between us, a whole generation; I was more than old enough to be his mother. The subject of the age difference had never been bought up and on the face of it he didn't seem fazed by it, but while we were out I was aware of being, shall we say, noticed and it was obvious what people were thinking when they looked at me and then at Garry.

Anyway I had known him for a respectable two weeks and tonight we were dining at my place. We had not as yet become sexually intimate and although I had invited him in for coffee on a number of occasions, all I received was a good night kiss on the doorstep prior to his departure. Mind you they were long lingering intimate kisses, on my instigation I might add, and last night as he pulled away his hand did gently caress my breast. Again on my instigation as I held his fore arm in such a way as he couldn't help but touch me. I gave him a knowing smile and he gave a nervous cough as he returned to his car. He was in many ways refreshingly old fashioned and that to some extent went to put my mind at ease about our age gap. He didn't volunteer much information about the break up of his marriage so I didn't press him on the subject; all that I knew was that she had left him for another man.

Tonight I decided to find out what he was made of. I insisted he came by taxi as I intended the wine to flow freely and if I did my seduction properly, it would be a one way journey. I had been a widow for five years and although I was nearing, or depending on your outlook, passed retiring age. I still had sexual desires, strong sexual desires, which had not been fulfilled since my poor husband sadly passed away.

I emerged from the shower and towelled myself dry. Standing in front of the mirror I surveyed my figure, not bad for my age I suppose. I had kept myself fit and trim and to some extent had warded off some of the ravages of time. My legs were a good shape and some simple surgery for thread veins last year was money well spent. My hips were quite broad, but I've been told that men like that, to which I heard someone whisper "more to grip onto when doing it from behind," which I suppose was a sort of a compliment. And my breasts were a good shape and reasonably firm, though quite small, which was probably for the best because large tits at my age would probably be hanging around my knees.

My hair was in a short, sort of round style that needed just a run through with the brush just to fluff it up and it was set for the evening. I sprinkled talc on my hands and caressed it into my body starting with my breasts. My nipples immediately became erect at the attention and were like firm ripe cherries as my fingers gently smoothed in the talc. I gave my breasts a lot of attention, feeling their contours and kneading them. Lifting them up and pushing them together, then releasing them and watching in the mirror as they resumed their position with a gentle bob.

Further on down I went, across my tummy and down to my pussy. I sprinkled more talc on my palm as I saved the best bit until last as I gently rubbed it between my legs. My vagina tingled as my fingers passed by, my middle finger just gently parting my lips ever so slightly and just as gently paying a passing compliment to my clitoris. 'Steady on old girl,' I thought to myself, 'save it till later.' You've been doing it yourself for five years; tonight will be the real thing. I dusted off the excess talc from between my legs and got dressed. I wore a long sleeved white blouse, which was of quite a thick material beautifully embroidered, with a high frilly collar tied with a wide white ribbon done up in a bow. A calf length dark full skirt complemented by high leg dark brown boots completed the ensemble. It was a variation of the outfit I wore on our first date and Garry was particularly complementary about it.

I went through to the kitchen to check on the meal. I was doing a Hungarian goulash. It was one of those dishes that could be prepared in advance and kept in a slow oven until it was needed and then just put on a plate. I had done some plain boiled potatoes to go with it which were in a covered bowl with a little water to keep warm. It was ready and smelt very good I must admit. All that was required now was the guest of the evening to work up an appetite. I closed the oven door and the door bell went, perfect timing. I felt my heart flutter a little and I went to answer the door, checking make up and hair in the hall mirror on the way past.

I opened the door and there stood Garry with an armful of flowers. How typical and how sweet of him. He was not a bad looking man; just less than six feet tall of medium build. A full set of thick curly hair that looked as though it would carry him through to middle age; my age, I sighed to myself. He had soft blue eyes and a complexion that easily blushed when he was agitated or embarrassed, but all things considered, a very good catch.

   'Not too late am I Sandra?' He said with that dimpled smile of his.
   'Not at all, in fact spot on. Come on in.'
   'For you.' He said.
   'Garry, they're lovely. Take a seat and I'll put them in a vase.'
   Garry settled himself on the settee as I went to the kitchen and quickly filled a vase and put the flowers in. I returned to the lounge and put them on the coffee table.

'They look really good Garry, thank you very much.'

'Mmm, something smells good.'

'Hungarian goulash, I hope that's OK.'

'Splendid, one of my favourites. You are looking very attractive tonight.'

'Thank you.'

'Dressed for the food.'

'I'm sorry.' I said a little confused.

'Your outfit, very eastern European, Hungarian, or even Russian.'

'Oh yes, I suppose it is. But it's purely coincidence.' I said flattered that he had noticed.

There seemed to be a sparkle in his eye tonight, a new sort of confidence. Perhaps this could be a night to remember I thought to myself. However this age difference was still concerning me, I felt I needed to clarify our situation. I was becoming very fond of Garry and I needed to know how he felt about the possibility of a relationship, maybe even a lifelong relationship. I decided to take the bull by the horns and tonight at the earliest opportune moment I would ask him.

'Would you like a drink?'

'Yes please.'

'Gin and tonic?'

'Gin and tonic would be splendid.'

I prepared the drinks and joined Garry on the settee. He sipped it approvingly.

'Garry,' I ventured, 'I've been thinking about our age difference.'

'Yes, I've been thinking about it too.' His voice lowered as he said it and I felt my heart drop. 'And you feel uncomfortable about it.' He continued with a slight tremble in his voice.

'No, not at all,' I emphasised, 'I just thought you might feel uncomfortable about going out with a woman of my age'.

'I feel proud to be going out with a woman of your age and I feel privileged that you have consented to let me court you. Age means nothing to me, I want you for yourself.'

His sincerity affected me emotionally. 'I don't know what to say Garry, that was a really wonderful complement.' I could feel tears of joy welling up in my eyes and Garry sensing the mood took me in his arms.

'I've only known you for a few short weeks Sandra and in that time I've come to realise that you are the one for me. If you believe in love at first sight, well this is the living proof.'

We held each other tightly and the emotional aura was unbelievable. We had both had similar worries and now they were washed away, we were as one. He lifted my chin with his finger and my watery eyes looked into his. He caught a tear rolling down my cheek with his finger and gently brushed it away. We held a gaze of wonderment and slowly our lips came together and we kissed gently. Our kiss continued and a passion was beginning to blossom. It blossomed into fruition and our passion became inflamed. We kissed with greater urgency and I could feel Garry's strong arms grip my body. The electricity was flowing with more power and I could sense the sexual passion within. His kissing was more urgent and our mouths were open receiving each others tongues in turn. His hand was gently but firmly travelling across my back and under my arm and I sensed his breathing was becoming deeper. This was it, I knew where his hand was going and I wanted him to take my breast. I felt his hand gently follow the outline of my breast then he gripped it more firmly as his breathing became hotter and more urgent. I felt my cheeks flush with sexual passion. His hands tantalised and teased my yearning breast. He kissed my neck and down my chest until his eager mouth found my nipple. He sucked it through the fabric of my blouse while continuing to fondle it with his strong hands, he kissed me again and his tongue erotically licked the top of my mouth. My pussy was beginning to tingle and I knew what it wanted. The time was right and I took him by the hand and led him to the bedroom.

I closed the door and threw my arms around his neck and kissed him again. I pushed him away and stepped back from him. He just stood and stared and breathed heavily. Unfastening my belt and clasp my skirt fell away. Garry gasped at what he saw. I leaned against the dressing table and was about to unzip my boots.

'No.' He commanded. 'Leave them on.'

He gazed at me in wonderment and I knew he could see that tantalising white triangle of my knickers just below the level of my blouse. That tantalising white triangle that covered the greatest wonder of the world as far as men were concerned. Slowly I unfastened my ribbon around my neck and slowly and seductively unbuttoned my blouse. I looked up at Garry with a seductive eye and he gently licked his lips, obviously wondering what delights lay within. Gently I let it slide from my shoulders to reveal a skimpy white bra that showed off my small bust to perfection. In my white underwear and boots I walked slowly towards my man.

Putting my hands on his pounding chest they moved up to scoop his grey sports jacket from his shoulders, his keys and coins jangled as it hit the floor. His tie unfastened flew over my shoulder. Unbuttoning his shirt revealed an almost hairless but full chest, not muscular exactly but pleasant and inviting to snuggle up against on a cold winters evening. I brushed it from his shoulders like his jacket. He stood obediently as I unfastened and unzipped his trousers and let them fall about his ankles. He smoothly removed them and his shoes and socks in one movement. Not something that can always be done gracefully, but he managed it beautifully. There we both stood, in our underwear. I could feel my vagina becoming wet in anticipation of the pleasures to come, and I also noticed a stirring within Gary's shorts. He held his arms open and I went to him and it felt as though I was just scooped up like a doll in his strong arms. He kissed me gently and lovingly, slowly building into a greater passion. I felt the taut muscles of his back and I felt I wanted this man, I wanted his body to worship mine, and I wanted to be whipped up into a frenzy of sexual turmoil. I knew nothing of his sexual preferences so had no idea what he had planned. As we kissed I felt the throbbing of his manhood against my tummy and I wanted it inside me, taking me to erotic heights, filling me with the epitome of sexual pleasure. My pussy was soaked with love juice and it wanted attention. His hands slid up my back and he unclipped my bra. I let him pull it from me and I felt my breasts gently sway as they were given their freedom. Garry gasped as he saw them.

'They are perfect.' He said with a sigh of pleasure

He fondled and sucked them with the greatest of reverence. It excited me greatly and it also fascinated me how much men worshiped breasts. It was probably something to do with the mother bonding instinct I thought, but whatever it was I was glad that my breasts were giving him such great pleasure. He continued with his worship for a few minutes longer then his lips met mine again for more fevered and passionate kissing. He paused and stepped back, putting his thumbs into his shorts and pushed them down. As he did so his shaft sprung up like a ramrod. It was hard and stiff and ready for action and I was ready to give it some. As he stepped out of his shorts he took me in his arms again. I began to kiss his chest and kissed lower and lower down across his abdomen. I now kneeled before him to worship his shaft. I took it in my tiny hand and gently let it slide up and down the length of his shaft.

'Oh god.' He moaned in pleasure.

I held it before me and kissed the end, then opened my mouth and let it slip between my lips, feeling the large ridge of his shaft enter me. I gently sucked him and let it slide out again. Then let my lips travel over his shaft end again and this time I took it in further gently sucking. Pulling back again and feeling his ridge passing by my lips. He was obviously in raptures and I wasn't really sure how far I should go. I had never really been keen on the idea of going all the way and taking his semen in my mouth but if it was what he wanted I would do it. I continued to suck him for another few strokes then Garry took control. He took my arms and pulled me to my feet and kissed me putting his tongue in my mouth where his cock had been seconds before.

'Your turn now.' He said and sat me on the edge of the bed. Pushing me back he took hold of my knickers and I raised my hips a little and let him slide them off. He kneeled on the floor between my parted legs. My vagina tingled and I felt my lips quivering for him. He kissed my knee and slowly kissed the inside of my thigh getting higher and higher towards the ultimate goal. I lifted my legs high and wide, holding them with my hands behind my thighs to give Garry maximum access to my womanhood. Garry's hands caressed the back of my thighs and I felt his thumbs part my lips even wider. His lips found my lips and his tongue found my clitoris. I screamed with pleasure as he licked me. He licked me gently and rhythmically and it was overwhelmingly wonderful. I was aware I was losing control and moaning and screaming loudly. He licked me harder, backwards and forwards and it was becoming too good to be true. Orgasm was just a few tongue strokes away and I could feel the momentum building inside me. It was taking me over. Garry knew I was on the verge and he taunted me cruelly. I just wanted one more lick and the roller coaster of pleasure would take over me. He gave me that last lick and I screamed out and shook as I erupted into uncontrollable pleasure. He licked me harder and faster and the feeling was unbelievable and could not be stopped, even if I wanted to. On and on he licked and on and on went the grip of pleasure. It took over mind and body and seemed to go on forever. As it levelled out Garry changed his licking to sucking and he sucked my clitoris and my labia, almost as if he was sucking out my love juice. It was different, it was beautiful, and it was earth shatteringly wonderful.

I was breathless and exhausted, but it wasn't over yet. Garry swept me up in his strong arms and lay me in the middle of the bed. He got on top of me and I wrapped my legs around him and I felt his shaft slide inside me. I felt that enormous purple ridge that had been in my mouth was now sliding between another set of lips. It was brilliant and I felt his huge cock penetrate me deeply. He thrust with great vigour and I could feel my tits shaking as he fucked me. I dug my heels into the back of my stallion, urging him to thrust inside me deeper and faster. On and on he went and I could tell he was not far off. He thrust harder and faster and I could feel his shaft hit the top of my tunnel of love. He cried out as he came, his shaft pulsing his hot semen into my welcoming little cunt.

To say it was a mind blasting experience, is an understatement of what that night was like, but words are not nearly adequate enough to describe it. I sincerely hope that our relationship will blossom and we will have many more nights like this.

And on a final note the Hungarian goulash was pretty good too.

LOVE AT LAST

⚭

I was feeling very nervous; this was my first night as a teacher. Not only my first night as a teacher but a teacher thrown in at the deep end, because this was to be a new untried course, with an accreditation for the successful students at the end of it. It was a course in international cuisine. Why am I doing it I asked myself, well for a number of reasons? On the positive side cooking was my passion, unfortunately so was eating as my expanding figure will testify. On the negative side I had a full time day job which I hated and didn't pay well, plus, it had little or no promotion possibilities. I was thirty years old and a single mother, so my matrimonial aspirations looked bleak as well. The few men that I did date dropped me like a hot brick when they found out about Susan. I was in a no win situation, I loved my daughter dearly and I should be spending more time with her, but the mortgage had to be paid so I needed every penny I could get. So here I was awaiting the arrival of my first class.

For the first night I had planned to cook a Moroccan lamb Tagine, but even before I started I had made a foul up. I had forgotten to bring any honey. Well too late now, I had to go with what I had. I looked at the class register and there were only four names on it. Which meant there was the possibility that the class is likely to fizzle out with such a poor attendance, but on the other hand, with my inexperience, the smaller the class the better. I looked through the names, Linda Bell, Simon

Richmond and John and Sarah Billings, a husband and wife team I thought.

There were still a few minutes to go so I made a final check of my ingredients etc. I would be demonstrating the cooking of the lamb tagine, then hand out the recipe at the end of the lesson and the class would cook it next week. Then I would give them the recipe for the following week and so on. I went to check in the store room, just in case by some stroke of luck there was some honey, but alas none. There was a full length mirror in there, so I checked my appearance, hoping at least that I had the veneer of a chef. My hair was nearly shoulder length with a fringe. It was, I have to admit a bit thin and lifeless. My face was ordinary enough, not ugly, just plain. And my figure, well, a love of cooking and eating reflected in its shape. My backside was bordering on over large and the decision to wear skin tight ski pants was not a good one. I must remember to wear a skirt in the future. I was also wearing a thin woollen top which showed off my only attractive asset, a huge sixty three inch bust. This seemed to be the main thing that attracted men to me. It has always been large, but becoming overweight and having had a child, increased its size enormously. I held in my stomach and stuck out my chest and adjusted my breasts in my bra so they were at least level. My nerves, combined with my caressing, had made my nipples become erect, which were also larger than normal and they protruded from my thin clingy top almost indecently. I put my apron on quickly to partially cover myself up and hoped they would subside before the class arrived.

I walked back into the kitchen classroom as the first student arrived, a tall man of medium build, with a very distinguished head of graying hair. He had a managerial air about him and I must admit I found him very attractive. I wonder if this is part of the husband and wife team, I thought.

'Hello there. Are you John or Simon?' I asked.

'I'm Simon.' He said offering his hand'

'I'm Claire.' I replied.

He seemed to hold my hand for an awfully long time and as he did so his sparkling blue eyes gazed into mine. I felt my heart pound and my cheeks begin to flush.

'Well you're the first to arrive,' I said, 'so take your pick of the cookers.'

'Right, er, thank you,' he said, somewhat unsure of himself, 'I'm afraid they are all the same to me though.'

'Not done much cooking then?'

'Very little, in fact since my wife passed away I've been living on baked beans, microwave meals and take-aways.'

My heartbeat began to rise again. I'm almost ashamed to say, that this man, twenty years my senior really attracted me. But then I thought why should I be ashamed, age means nothing, after all we are both free agents. I bought myself back to reality.

'Well I'm sure when you have completed the course; you will be competent enough to knock up a Spaghetti Bolognese or a Chilli con Carne.'

Another student arrived. 'Hello I'm Claire.'

'Hi, I'm Linda.' She replied.

'Just two more to come and we'll get started.' And at my very words John and Sarah arrived. Not husband and wife, as I supposed, but mother and son. Anyway the first evening was a success and everyone enjoyed the meal I prepared, even without the honey.

All through the following week until the next class I found myself thinking of Simon, I just couldn't get him out of my mind. All sorts of possible scenarios ran through my brain. I fancied him like mad. But what if I wasn't his type; would I end up making a fool of myself and cause huge embarrassment?

The following week the class were all busy preparing their ingredients and I sidled up to Simon. 'That's looking good Simon.' I said.

'The chopping is a bit uneven I'm afraid.'

'Nothing to worry about, after all this is a rustic dish.'

I leaned forward to put next week's recipe sheet in his folder, and as

I did so I let my breasts rub against his upper arm. Being the gentleman he was, he just moved away slightly.

I let them all get on with their cooking and I caught up with my paper work. I had to admit, I felt a little depressed. I was trying my best to attract Simon without being too obvious, but he never seemed to rise to the bait. I began to think that he thought of me like all the others did, an overweight ageing frump with a kid. But I couldn't help thinking about that first night and that penetrating look that he gave me, that look that seemed to communicate so much.

Anyway later that evening fate was to take a hand. Simon and I were the last to leave and we loaded our cars. To my horror it wouldn't start. Simon noticed my plight and came to offer his help. 'Dead as a Dodo.' I said.

'Is there anything I can do?'

Anyway he looked at the engine but could do nothing to get it started. In the meantime I phoned my brother, who was a mechanic, but he was out on a job and it would be over an hour before he could get to me. My next thought was for Susan. She was staying with my parents for the evening; I phoned to tell them about my dilemma. My dilemma was their salvation and they eagerly offered to keep Susan overnight. I knew Susan would love it, as my parents spoiled her terribly, and they loved having her to themselves. Someone once said that there is a great bond between grandparents and grandchildren because they share a common enemy. A bit of an over statement, but I got their meaning. So two of my problems were sorted.

'Can I give you a lift home?' Asked Simon.

'If it's no trouble, I would be very grateful.' I replied, relieved that my third problem was now hopefully being resolved.

'No trouble whatsoever.' He said with a slightly wicked twinkle in his eye.

Things were looking promising.

We pulled up outside my house. 'Would you like to come in for a coffee?' I asked.

Simon hesitated. Oh no, I thought, he's going to turn me down.
'I would love to.'
A wave of relief swept over me; at last I will have him alone.

Well here we were alone at last. Thoughts raced through my mind, shall
I play the tart and lead him on, or shall I let him take the initiative.
One thing I was convinced of was tonight has got to be the night, if he
walked out of that door without our relationship being consummated,
then that would be it. I decided to go with the flow at first and if he made
movements to leave I would take drastic measures even ripping my bra
off and smothering him with my tits if necessary.
'Would you like a cup of coffee Simon, or perhaps you would prefer
tea?'
'Coffee would be fine thank you.'
I went through to the kitchen and filled the kettle, Simon followed
me through.
'Nice kitchen.' He said.
'Not bad, a bit small, but for now it will have to do.'
The phone rang and I answered it on the mobile. 'Hello... Oh great,
well that's a relief, thanks very much... One of the students gave me a
lift... thanks once again, I'll see you tomorrow.' I put the phone down
and returned to the coffee preparation. 'That was my brother; he's picked
up the car and will sort it out in the morning.'
'Good. It's useful having someone like that in the family.'

I went to the cupboard for a couple of mugs and had to squeeze past the
island and Simon to reach it. As I went past I felt my breasts rub against
him and I stopped momentarily. Simon put his hand on my shoulder and
stared into my eyes in exactly the same way he did on the first night of
the course. And now, as then, I felt that same pounding in my heart and
the same flush of my cheeks. Fuck the coffee I thought, this is it. Simon
took my chin with his other hand and lifted my head, we came closer and
closer and our lips met. I felt myself melting as his arms wrapped around
me and he hugged me tightly. We kissed long and gently.
'I've wanted to do that for ages.' He said.
'And I've wanted you to do that for ages.' I replied.

He smiled at me and kissed me again, this time with more passionate urgency and I knew this was it. My theory was confirmed as I felt his hands slide from my back to my tummy and inevitably upwards. As he still kissed me I felt him sigh with pleasure as his hands took both my breasts. He fondled and kissed desperately for a few seconds then took me in his arms and hugged me with my head on his shoulder.

'Oh Claire.' He murmured gently.

I pushed him away gently and took hold of his hand. 'Come on,' I said demurely, 'I'll show them to you.'

In the bedroom he stood like a statue as I unbuttoned and removed my shirt. With equal smoothness I kicked off my shoes and let my skirt fall to the floor. I stepped out of it and I stood before him in my bra and panties. He stared longingly at my cleavage, my huge tits bursting to get out. Sixty three inches of heaving breasts contained inside a garment that trussed them up, stopped them wobbling about and reduced their size. They were about to receive their freedom for Simon's delight. I reached around my back and unclipped my bra and I felt my breasts sag. I crossed my arms over my chest and took my shoulder straps and literally tore my bra off and threw it across the room to reveal my greatest assets in all their magnificence. I put my hands on my chest and let them gently flow over my breasts. I lifted them up and pushed them together letting Simon drool over the cleavage. Then I just shook them from side to side like a whore, two huge mounds of tit flesh shaking and wobbling and wanting attention.

He was speechless and still like a statue seemingly unable to take in the majesty of the sight. I walked over to him and unbuttoned and removed his shirt, followed quickly by his trousers and shoes. All that was left was his shorts and I could see from the bulge that I would not be disappointed with their contents. Gently and slowly I eased them down to reveal his erect cock. I was right I wasn't disappointed, it was large thick and as stiff as iron and ready for action. I decided in my mind that I would not keep it waiting. I took his hand once more and led him to the bed. 'Lie down Simon.' I instructed. He did so and as he lay there I kneeled beside him and let my breasts dangle over his shaft, teasing him mercilessly as I let them sway back and forth tormenting his cock. By now I was more than ready for it, my cunt was feeling very juicy and it wanted Simons's stiff cock inside it. I positioned myself across Simon, kneeling either side of his hips and taking his big purple ended cock I guided it between my lips. I gasped and sighed as I felt this mighty warrior slide inside me. I gently lowered myself onto his cock and was in ecstasy as I felt it penetrating my womanhood. I sank down low onto him and I could feel his shaft reach the top of my cunt as it poked hard inside me. Simon moaned with pleasure as I raised my hips higher then dropping down hard onto him to force his cock as far and as hard inside my cunt as I could and at the same time letting my tits shake about for him. After a few more thrusts I changed my technique and came down on Simon taking his full length. Then I moved my hips backwards and forwards so that I rubbed my clitoris against his pelvic bone, that, and his pubes tickling me made a surge of ecstasy rush through my body. To give myself greater control I rested my hands on his chest, this having the added benefit of letting my breasts dangle and shake right above Simon's face and he couldn't take his eyes off them. As I rocked back and forth my clit rubbing against his body, Simon was making me build up to what was going to be an explosive orgasm. Also what added to the pleasure was that I could feel Simon's cock deep inside me and with my gyrating hips; it stretched my cunt one way then the other. I was beginning to feel myself coming. I sat up straight and put my left hand on my hip and with the other hand I reached down to finger my clit. This gave me greater control and I felt Simons's thick hard cock stretching my lips apart. I gyrated my hips faster and fingered my clitoris to the point of no return. Simon was moaning and his face was contorted with pleasure, he too was on the verge of a climactic orgasm.

'Fuck me harder Claire, fuck me harder.' He begged.

I obliged him and fucked him so hard I worried that I might break off his cock. I need not have worried because it seemed to take on an even greater size and hardness inside me.

He kept his eyes on my tits which because of my position and my frantic gyrations were bouncing up and down and banging together. What a sight it must have looked for Simon sixty three inches of rampant tit flesh bouncing for his delight. On and on I thrust and the ecstasy was taking over me, I was coming. I could feel my cunt tightening and sucking Simon's throbbing cock and as I sucked him I could feel his cock pulsate. We orgasmed together, it was beautiful, we both screamed out our pleasure. I felt Simon's hot semen pump into me and at the same time my cunt, like a hungry mouth, sucked it from him. I carried on fucking him and my cunt squelched as Simon's semen oozed out of me. The orgasm gradually subsided and I remained kneeling over Simon with his shaft still inside me. I felt tears of joy rolling down my cheeks and Simon lay there exhausted.

I am happy to say that Simon was very different to all the others and we are having a long and meaningful relationship and all is wonderful with the world. Susan loves him like a father and you're probably not really interested but I've managed to get a decent job thanks to Simon's contacts.

WEEKEND DREAM

It was Friday evening and I had just arrived home from work. I was glad the week was over, it had been one of those traumatic weeks when everything that could go wrong, did go wrong. Still, all the aggravation had not been in vain, we had a tight schedule to meet and we achieved it. Mostly due to me I might add, but I don't suppose my achievements will be acknowledged, or even recognised. The upper echelons are always quick to seize the credit for a job well done, but are equally and negatively efficient at dumping the shit on anyone who makes a mistake, or anyone who they can use as a scapegoat for their own balls ups. I'm sure everyone recognises their career pattern somewhere amongst that little lot so I won't bore you with it any further. Suffice to say it looks better now it's behind me, so on with the good life.

The front door shut behind me, I walked through to the lounge, kicked off my crippling stilettos, threw my jacket over the back of the chair and went straight to the fridge and got out the bottle of Chardonnay that I had started last night. All I wanted now was a night of gentle relaxation. David had been working away all week and would be home tomorrow and I yearned for his company. I hated it when he worked away, especially on a week like the one I have just had to endure. It didn't seem to matter however bad things got, it was always reassuring to know he was at home to comfort me. Anyway I decided to have an early night and tomorrow I would make an early start with the shopping and get something extra special for dinner tomorrow night. I might even treat myself to some exotic lingerie to spice up his evening.

I took my glass of wine and the rest of the bottle and went upstairs for a shower. I went into the bedroom, looked at the bed and sighed, it's been a big empty bed this week, but come tomorrow night it will be a shrine of unrestrained lechery. I stripped off all my clothes and just dropped them where they fell and stood naked looking at myself in the full length mirror at the foot of the bed. We had mirrors all around the room and I must admit it added a decidedly spicy facet to having sex when you could actually see yourself being fucked. It was like watching a porno film with yourself as the star. To complement the one at the foot of the bed we had one at the head and it was incredible to see the multiple reflections, because it looked as though you were looking down a tunnel of ever diminishing images of sex. David had even suggested having one on the ceiling, but I thought that was a bit too much. I took my breasts in my hands and kissed my nipples in turn, then sucked them to make them erect. Not bad I thought, and still quite firm. I shook them about, David loved it when I did that, he seemed to have a fascination about my tits shaking about (don't they all). If we were having sex and I was on top of him taking control I always exaggerated my movements so they would bounce with abandon, and the sight of them always made him more rampant.

I lay on the bed for a few moments and opened my legs, and dreamed of our past sexual adventures. Remembering my wine I sat up and drained the glass and caught sight of myself in the mirror. That was the image I presented to David to turn him on, me lying naked on the bed with my legs open. Then when he stood there gasping I slowly slid my hands down my belly and between my legs, gently pulling my lips open for him so he could see my tunnel of love, a pleasure palace that was aching for his attention. I lay back on the bed and sighed, I could feel the effects of the wine and my mind began to drift, the fresh evening breeze caressed my body and I felt myself sliding into slumber. I slowly floated and drifted down through cotton wool clouds falling deeper and deeper into an incredibly relaxing deep, deep sleep. Waves of comfort flowed over me. Veils of silk descended from the ceiling and covered my naked body like luxurious sheets, while in the distance I heard the sounds of flowing water and the distant gentle strumming of a harp. Down and down I drifted through the levels of sleep, heavenly sleep, beautiful relaxing sleep.

A heavy door latch lifted and the huge riveted oak door creaked open. Clouds of ethereal mist drifted into the room and when it began to clear, David stood before me in a white robe that gently wrapped his athletic body and flowed over his left shoulder. On his head a laurel wreath in solid gold that caught a shaft of sunlight from the window and its multi facets lit up the room in a soft, misty gold light. He pulled the robe from his shoulder and as he stared at me silently, he released it and it seemed to unravel from his body and fall to the floor. He was naked and beautiful wearing nothing but his gold crown of laurel. His body was perfect and like his crown seemed to give out a golden glow. His shoulders were broad and muscular as were his arms, his sinews like whipcord and his veins like rope. He had a trim narrow waist, with a perfect battery of taut stomach muscles, narrow hips that sported tight muscular buttocks, thick strong thighs like boughs of trees and legs with runner's calves. And between thighs and waist was the best of all, a scrotum the size of a fist, contained testicles that a prize Hereford bull would be proud of. His shaft hung with all the majesty you would expect from such a man. It was six inches long and tremendously thick and as he walked closer to the bed it waved slowly from side to side. I could not take my eyes from it, the movement of his muscular thighs pushed his whole manly suite from side to side, his balls shuffling their position within the confines of his scrotum. He stood before me and his hand took his mighty shaft in its palm and half closing his hand he slowly and gently stroked its length, his huge purple knob end almost seemed to glow. His whole shaft within a few seconds was swelling up to its maximum. The sight transfixed me and his manhood had gone from a soft six inches up to a rock hard throbbing ten inches of pulsating cock flesh. But what was so outstanding was the size of his knob end, it was the size of a lemon and the ridge was a good half inch wider all the way round than the rest of his very thick shaft.

He stood at the foot of the bed and serenely waved his arm slowly over it and the silken sheets gently flew away to reveal my naked body lying there. I raised my knees and opened my legs. I could feel my lips were beginning to tingle with the thoughts of what was about to become me. My hands automatically glided down my belly and between my legs and I gently caressed my lips for David's pleasure. With a gesture of his hand he bade me to sit up and I obediently sat on the edge of the bed to await his desire. He pushed his knee between mine and I opened my legs, he then put his other knee there and opened his legs to force mine even wider. He gently put his left hand behind my head while his other hand presented me with his huge ramrod of a cock. I took it in my hands and gently kissed the end. It was huge and I wanted it. I opened my mouth as wide as I could and took it in, just barely able to take his bulbous cock end. I felt his hand behind my head urging me to take more, but it was impossible my mouth was stretched to its maximum and I could take no more. I sucked what I could and with my hand I rubbed his shaft up and down. After a few minutes I could hear him breathing heavily, his cock end still in my mouth and I continued rubbing its length with my hand. His hips were thrusting, trying to force more of his cock into my mouth and I felt his huge bell end swelling and his shaft pulsating, David was coming. He let out a long cry and moments later I felt his hot semen surge into my mouth filling it completely. I pulled away still rubbing his shaft, semen oozing from my mouth and still ejaculating out of his cock in cascading spurts. It shot over my cheeks and almost covered my face. It was magnificent and as I continued to jerk him off he just kept coming. I pointed it at my tits and within seconds they too were both covered in strands of sticky semen. Eventually the last drop was squeezed out onto my breasts.

But David was not finished yet. He gestured me to turn over and I kneeled on the edge of the bed. He stood behind me and again his legs forced mine apart, this time very widely. I was kneeling on the edge with my legs stretched to their widest. I felt his hands on my buttocks and his cock was nuzzling against my pussy lips. I felt them begin to part as his cock eased its way inside me. I felt them stretch as I felt that huge knob end enter me and I felt the ecstasy of its rim rub the inside of my cunt. Gently onwards it slid until it reached its ultimate penetration, or should I say my ultimate penetration, because looking in the mirror I could see David's shaft inside me and he had another two inches at least to go. David fucked me hard; I felt his cock ramming into me, right to the top of my cunt. It hurt but it was a beautiful hurt. David rammed harder and harder and in the mirror he still had two inches to spare and it seemed as if he was trying his damnedest to get those last two inches inside my overstretched cunt. On and on he continued to ram me, I could see my tits hanging down and shaking with every mighty thrust. It was agony and ecstasy at the same time. Eventually ecstasy took over and I could feel myself coming. I screamed out and David thrust even harder as he was coming in unison with me. My cunt sucked his cock, urging it on further inside me, I wanted his semen, and he obliged me. I felt his cock expand as he filled my cunt with his semen. I sucked him and thrust back against his thrusts. He gripped my hips with his strong hands and forced me onto his cock. My cunt was in turmoil, my body gripped with an unimaginably beautiful orgasm. I sucked him in and looking in the mirror, I took his last two inches inside me. The feeling was incredible and seemed to go on forever. David continued to thrust and I could feel and hear his semen as it poured and squelched out of me and ran down my thighs. Eventually it died down and silence fell, just our gentle breathing, we were both satisfied. David took a bottle of aromatic oil and poured a pool of it into his hands then massaged it into my feet. It was truly sensual and relaxing and he continued to massage my whole body. It was so relaxing I drifted, drifted, drifted, drifted, into a deep deep, deep, sleep.

In the distance the silence was broken by a strange warbling sound that seemed to echo around my head and seemed to come from nowhere. It seemed to get closer and louder. I was woken by the phone. In my confusion I pressed the speaker button and a voice said.

'Karen it's me'.

'David. You were wonderful.'

'What? Are you alright?'

'Wonderfully so. I've just had a marvellous dream about you.'

'Was it good?'

'You were excellent.'

A LIFT HOME

The factory was almost silent, just the occasional creak and hiss as the once vibrant machinery was beginning to cool down. An empty silent factory to me always took on an atmosphere of calm after the storm. Everyone had gone except Fiona and me, and she was about to leave too. I was just finishing off some paperwork as she came over. Fiona was a very quiet and shy woman of about twenty six, nothing special about her, she didn't stand out in a crowd, but I must admit I liked her very much. I had often thought about asking her out as I knew she was single, in fact divorced, with as far as I knew, no other love interest at the moment. And as I was single and of a similar age, we would I thought make a good match. The only thing that put me off was the fact that we worked together and I had always been wary of getting emotionally involved with someone I worked with. This phobia started many years ago when I first started work and fell in love for the first time with a girl in the office. I was seriously in love, but she was just playing around and indeed was seeing someone else at the same time. It became common knowledge within the company and there was the inevitable sniggering and leg pulling which I found very distressing and embarrassing. Needless to say the affair ended and I was left at an emotional disadvantage, shall we say. The embarrassing harassment continued and being a junior in a very large company I was unable to suppress it, so inevitably I left, vowing never to get involved with someone I worked with ever again. To bring my romantic history up to date I have found it difficult to let my emotions go, as there was always the fear of public humiliation, so there has not been anyone really serious since that fiasco.

Anyway, back to the present, Fiona was approaching with her bag in one hand and her coat in the other. She always walked with very small steps and almost slid her feet across the floor; in fact it was more of a shuffle than a walk and as her feet shuffled so did her shoulders. Whenever you caught her eye she always smiled and every conversation started with an 'Ooooh,' and was inevitably followed by a little laugh. A lot of the women were irritated by this and thought her a bit simple. Her supervisor Marion in particular gave her a hard time and spoke to her very abruptly, mind you there weren't many people that Marion didn't speak to abruptly. But Fiona was a good soul and a diligent worker. She was about five foot six and of very slim build, in fact she had very little shape to her hips. This was made up for however by a very ample, but discreet bust. I'm afraid discreet is the best word I have available, because although her bust seemed of good proportions, it wasn't advertised. Rather than being pushed up into a display of cleavage, it seemed to hang down, but in a controlled fashion, if you know what I mean.

Her hair style was classical and simple. She had long straight, shoulder length brown hair. The sides of which were gently gathered and fastened with a clasp behind her head and she had a wispy fringe that was cut into points. Beneath the fringe were big brown eyes and a slightly long, but not unpleasant face. In fact as she stood there dressed in a woollen lilac top with matching cardigan, calf length skirt and heavy brown Brogue shoes, she almost had an air of the landed gentry about her.

'Oooh, I'm going now Dave, I've packed the last box and put it in the loading bay.' She cooed and giggled.
    'Right. Thanks Fiona. I do appreciate what you've done.'
    I suddenly thought, here I am alone with her, shall I make my feelings known, shall I make a pass at her? I stood up and took a deep breath.
    'Fiona.' I said seriously.
    'Yes.' She said, stopped suddenly in her tracks.
    I put a hand on each shoulder and pulled her towards me. She looked

slightly taken aback. I knew what I wanted to do, but at the same time doubts ran through my mind. Go for it, I told myself. I leaned towards her lips to kiss her and at the last moment she turned her cheek towards me and giggled as I kissed her.

'Oooh Dave.' And she giggled some more. 'I'll see you on Monday.'

With that she walked away. I've blown it, I thought to myself. But then again at least I've kissed her cheek and she didn't know what my intensions were, so maybe another day, who knows. I sighed as I heard the door slam as she left. I finished off my paperwork then I locked up and left.

I hurried to my car as it was now pouring with rain, got in and drove off. A little way down the road I saw Fiona at the bus stop, she looked absolutely soaked. I pulled over and opened the window.

'Hop in, I'll take you home.'

'But I'm soaked and I'll wet your car.' She said with her face at the window, her hair soaked and the rain running down her face, her chin trembling with the cold.

'It will dry, now jump in.' I insisted.

She got in and it was obvious that she was soaked to the skin as she sat there shivering, rain drops falling from her hair.

I pulled away and she gave me directions to her home. I had known her for many years now, but I knew very little about her and as we talked I realised what a lot in common we had. The same type of music and love of walking in the countryside. We were about half a mile away from her house when disaster struck. There was a sudden dull thud and my vision was obscured by an enormous cloud of steam. Fortunately through the clouds I noticed a lay-by and managed to pull into it. I got out into the still pouring rain to inspect the damage and as I surveyed the scene my fears were confirmed. Fiona came to join me.

'What is it?' She asked.

'A radiator hose has split.' I sighed. 'I'm afraid that's it.'

'Well I live only half a mile down the road. Why don't you come and get dried off and ring the Auto Club from there when the rain stops.'

I accepted her offer and we walked the half mile to Fiona's house in the pouring rain. The journey only took about fifteen minutes at the most, but in that time I too was soaked to the skin. My feet were squelching in my shoes and I could feel droplets of water running down my back. It was a strange experience and although I was wet and cold physically, I felt a warm glow inside.

Fiona's house was like a romantic country cottage, and stood serenely in a tree lined lane. It looked lovely and inviting in the pouring rain and I tried to imagine it in its summer splendour. I paused at the gate to admire it.

'It's beautiful.' I said with the rain cascading down my face.

'Inherited from my parents. They were very much in love with it and with each other. When they passed away they died within forty eight hours of each other. Mum passed away peacefully in her sleep and Dad was so broken hearted that he followed her the same way soon after.'

'Oh I'm sorry.'

'Yes, it was very sad. But it was quite fitting really that they should go together; they were inseparable and I don't think either could have lived without the other. So here I am, an orphan. Gosh that sounds terrible doesn't it, me an orphan. You would think I was a little lost waif.'

As I looked at the rain pouring over her face that is exactly what she looked like; a little lost waif.

We stood at the gate looking into each others eyes. I felt that this was it; she was the woman for me. Working together or not, I was getting emotionally involved. I sensed she too was feeling the chemistry, gone had her oooh's and giggles and permanent smile. Here was a woman of smouldering passion. I took her shoulders and planted my lips firmly against hers. I slid my arms around her and squeezed her tightly feeling the wet from her sodden coat. She returned my affection and hugged me to her.

'Let's get inside,' she said, 'before we get pneumonia.'

She opened the gate and I followed her down the path. We went inside and the house was unbelievably beautiful and full of charm. Although I was soaked through the ambience was so warm it bought a glow to my heart. I took Fiona in my arms again and we kissed passionately and longingly. I felt at one with her and I wanted her in every respect. She still had her soaking coat on and I unbuttoned it and let my arm slide around her waist. We continued to kiss and I could feel sexual urges stirring within me. My arm gradually slid up her side until I found her breast. I cupped it delicately, feeling its contours and gently squeezing it. It felt firm and ample and she moaned gently as I fondled her. She pushed me away.

'We must get these wet things off.' She said seductively.

She took my hand and led me upstairs to the bedroom.

She released me in the doorway and she went into the room. She took off her cardigan and kicked off her shoes and in one slick movement she lifted off her lilac top. Then with a flick of the wrist her skirt was unfastened and in a soggy heap on the floor. She bent to pick up her wet clothes and as she did so I was able to see down her cleavage. Standing before me she was a picture. Her skin glistened with the wetness and although she still had on her underwear, because they were soaked, they were transparent and the whiteness of the material blended with her skin. She reached around her back and unclipped her bra, slowly and teasingly peeling it from her shoulders to reveal her breasts in all their glory. And heaven, how wonderful they were, with her having such a slender body they looked very large indeed. I couldn't take my eyes off them and she knew she had me spellbound and they swayed regally as she cast her bra aside. It was truly a sight to behold and I can't begin to tell you how it made me feel to see those gorgeous breasts there for my enjoyment. Fiona knew she was teasing me and had me in her power, she then removed the final frontier and slid down her transparent knickers to reveal the cutest pussy I have ever seen. Not shaven, but with very little hair, which revealed the fold of her pussy lips beautifully, and it was just waiting for me.

'You had better get out of those wet things.' She said in an unbelievably sexy voice.

I didn't need to be told twice and as I undressed she reached out a pile of towels. She gathered up her wet hair and wrapped it in a towel like a turban and at arms length with a larger towel she dried her back with a see sawing action at the same time letting her breasts bounce about to torment me. This shy cooing girl I had known all these years had turned into a tantalising sex siren. She then started to rub her breasts with the towel and it was almost too much for me as she pushed them up and together, and tantalisingly massaging them.

I was now down to my underpants and my erection was bulging out. Fiona had finished drying herself and my penis was aching with desire.

'Get them off.' She commanded.

I obeyed and my shaft twanged to attention as I peeled off my wet shorts.

'My, you are a big boy aren't you?'

I wasn't really, in fact I had always felt inadequate, but the compliment made me feel good. She slowly walked behind me with her towel and dried my back, moving the towel very slowly. Then down to my buttocks and fondling them more than drying them.

'Nice firm, thrusting buttocks.' I heard her whisper, which made my already stiff shaft, even stiffer.

She then slowly walked around to my front and dried my chest. Then slowly the towel went lower until it found my throbbing shaft. She rubbed it gently then put the towel aside and knelt down in front of me, sitting on her feet. She took my shaft in her hand and guided it into her mouth. I looked down in amazement as it gradually slid in and out of her mouth. It was a fantastic sight watching her mouth slide up and down my shaft as she gently held my hips. I moaned in supreme pleasure, it was unbelievable, it was too good. She paused and licked the end of my shaft.

'Would you like me to take you all the way?' She asked in a slow sexy voice.

I repeated that question to myself, not quite able to take in its magnitude.

'Would you like me to take you all the way Dave?' She repeated in the same manner.

Even hearing her say that, was almost enough to make me come.

'Oh yes please.' I begged.

She took my shaft in her mouth again and holding my hips she began to suck me again. I was so worked up I knew it would not take long. And I was right, after a few seconds sucking I could feel an unbelievable surge of pleasure and I knew I had reached the point of no return. I felt my cock throb as my semen surged through it and filled Fiona's mouth. She sucked harder and harder as I shot into her. As I looked down I could see my shaft covered in semen as Fiona took it in and sucked it off. It was an unbelievable experience and one that I had never had before. After a few more seconds I was a spent force. Fiona got to her feet and smiled, wiping a trickle of semen from the corner of her mouth with her finger.

'Did you enjoy that?'

'It was unbelievably beautiful.'

She took me by the hand and led me to the bed. With a gesture of her hand she invited me to lie down and she went into the en-suite emerging with a bowl which she placed on the dressing table. From it she removed a flannel which she squeezed almost dry, then kneeling on the bed she washed my sticky shaft. She did it so slowly and gently, it was sensual, made all the more so by the gentle swaying of her breasts. This process went on for a few minutes and the warmth of the flannel was very exotic. After the prolonged washing she dried me off with a warm towel, all the time those beautiful breasts were urging me on; in fact I was becoming aroused again.

Fiona got up and pulled a stool out from under the dressing table. She reached into the bowl and squeezed out the flannel again. Then she put her foot on the stool and slowly and seductively began to wash her pussy. She did it slowly and teasingly and gently moaned with pleasure as she did so. Again after a few minutes of watching this I was becoming erect again and Fiona knew she was pleasing me. She then wrung out the flannel and twisted into a roll then to my amazement she parted her pussy lips and slid the flannel inside her, pushing it in as far as it could go then pulling it back and repeating the motion. It was unbelievable sight to see and it was obviously giving her as much pleasure doing it as it was giving me watching her. She was moaning with pleasure as she pulled it out and put it in the bowl.

I could stand no more, I was fully erect again and I wanted her and I wanted her now. I jumped off the bed and took her in my arms. I kissed her with a passion that frightened me. I took her breasts, not gently this time but like a beast possessed and groped and fondled them wantonly. Fiona writhed and moaned in my arms.

'Take me.' She begged.

I scooped her up in my arms and carried her to the bed and threw her into the middle. I parted her legs and kneeled between her thighs. I manoeuvred myself until my shaft nuzzled against her pussy lips then pushed it into her. Her lips parted as my shaft went in and Fiona moaned and she wrapped her legs around my waist. It was an incredible feeling and her cunt felt wonderful, it was a tight fit, but that made it all the more pleasurable. I felt my shaft slide under her cervix as it penetrated deeply inside her. I kneeled and reached down and I lifted her hips so I could thrust into her with the maximum penetration. It was amazing and I could see my shaft slide into her and as I pulled out, her cunt lips sucked the sides of my shaft. Fiona moaned and squealed as I rammed my shaft into her. I held her hips and at each thrust pulled her hard onto me to get that extra bit inside her. I was like an animal and I fucked her hard and rough, my thrusting making her tits shake uncontrollably. Fiona reached down with her finger and stimulated her clitoris. It was an erotic sight to see and she whipped herself into a frenzy of ecstasy. I continued to slam my shaft into her and she continued to finger her clitoris. I couldn't take much more and I could feel myself coming and I cried out in abandoned pleasure. 'Oh Fiona, I'm coming.'

'Go for it David. Fuck me hard and fill my cunt with your hot come.'

Those words were enough to tip me over the edge and I felt myself explode into orgasm and I indeed filled her tight little cunt with my hot come. She screamed as she climaxed, and I felt her cunt tighten around my cock and suck the semen out of me. It seemed to be endless. This welter of supreme pleasure took me over and I was out of control. She too was overcome with ecstasy and we entered nirvana together. Eventually it died down and we lay panting and exhausted in each others arms and fell into a lover's slumber

LOVE ON THE PHONE

It was ten o'clock in the morning and I was still lying in bed. As there was no particular reason to dive out and launch myself into a frenzy of action, I lay there, feeling depressed. I was using up the last of this years holiday allocation and I now realised that I had not chosen my days wisely. Geoff had been called away somewhere up north to repair a conveyor system or something. Apparently the problem had virtually bought production to a standstill and men were being paid to stand around reading the paper. Geoff was the only engineer available, so drew the only short straw and to make matters worse, what was to be a two hour job, escalated into something bigger that necessitated an overnight stay.

I had hoped for two days of pure unadulterated sexual bliss, but that was now not going to happen. What also added to the general feeling of gloom was the fact that it had been raining solidly for two days and the forecast for the near future was far from favorable. I sighed mournfully and just lay there watching the rain trickle down the window.

I decided to salvage what I could of the day, positive thinking was the thing. I would start by having an invigorating shower, then nip into town and book the summer vacation. Looking out of the window I wondered if it would not be wiser to leave the shower until later. The rain was hammering down and the spray from passing cars was like a ground mist.

Mr. Cooper from three doors down, was hurrying back home with his dog, both absolutely soaked. The dog seemed to be enjoying the weather and was trying to splash through every puddle he could find. Mr. Cooper on the other hand looked far from amused and kept tugging at the dog's lead impatiently. I decided that the trip to town could wait until the weather improved. Therefore I just took on board the first part of plan 'A' and decided to have the shower.

I lifted my nightie over my head and let my tits shake free. If Mr. Cooper had looked up now he would have seen a sight to take his mind off the weather. I have to admit, I was quite proud of my figure, maybe a little bit of excess flesh here and there, but not too much. In fact Geoff always complained when I went on a diet because it used to come off my bust first. So I was happy to oblige, because I enjoyed my food and if Geoff was happy with my shape, then I was happy also.

I stood in front of the mirror and inspected my body. I had blond hair that was parted in the middle and was cut to curl around at jaw level. It was cut shorter at the back and layered in two tiers and with a full fringe at the front cut in spikes. I had big blue eyes and a baby face, as Geoff called it, with a little turned up nose that completed an elfin appearance (again Geoff's words). I let my hands run over my breasts, they were big and full and they really turned Geoff on. He also took a childish delight in fondling them and took an even greater delight in watching me fondle them. One of his favourite things was making me caress and massage them. It would really get him worked up. So much so, that his greatest delight was to jerk himself off and come all over my tits. It used to turn me on watching him do it, and I used to love to watch his explosive ejaculation and see the jets of semen shoot over my tits. He would squeeze every last drop out then spread it over my tits and nipples with his big purple bell end until my tits glistened under a coating of his hot semen. I sighed with pleasure at the thought of it and I could feel a warm moist tingle inside my slit. I had often wondered about this all consuming fascination men seem to have with breasts. I didn't understand it, but I was glad of it and used it to my advantage many times.

My sexual daydream was abruptly halted by the telephone ringing.

'Hello.'

'Hi Shirley, it's me.'

'Geoff.'

'How are you?'

'I was just thinking about you.'

'Good, it's nice to know I'm not forgotten. Listen, I've managed to get finished early and the frozen chickens are flying again.'

'Are you there now?'

'No I'm back in the motel room getting packed. I'm just about to have a shower then I'm on my way home.'

The thought of this raised my spirits immensely and I had a naughty idea. 'What have you got on?' I asked.

'Just a robe.' He answered, somewhat puzzled.

'Take it off.' I demanded.

'What?'

'Take it off and lie on the bed. I'm going to make it worthwhile you having a shower.'

'Wow.' Gasped Geoff and I heard the bed springs creak. 'What are you doing that end?'

'I'm lying naked on the bed and I've just reached something out of the bedside drawer.'

'The top drawer.' He gasped and I could almost see his mouth open in awe.

'Yes, the top drawer.' I answered seductively. It was here that I kept my vibrator. Ten inches of thick, veined, pulsating, vibrating plastic pleasure.

'Go on then. Switch it on and do it to yourself.' He said with panting eagerness.

'Not so fast big boy. You've got to suffer first.'

This feeling of power was unbelievable, I was feeling really horny and I wanted to get myself off, but I knew if I extended the beautiful torture the end result would be much greater. I heard Geoff panting over the phone. 'Now Geoff I want you to put your right hand on your chest.'

'Done that.' He said hastily.

'Slowly move it down your stomach.'

'Yes.'

'Slowly.' I barked.

'Yes, slowly.' He whimpered.

'Now take your balls in your hand.'

'Oh God.'

'And gently roll them around. Now how does that feel?'

'Like you are doing it.'

'Good. Now take your cock in your fist and gently caress it.'

'Oh Shirley I'm aching for it. Let me jerk myself off.'

'Not so fast big boy, you must wait. Don't you know its good manners to let a lady come first?' I felt the power and I knew Geoff's cock was nearly ready to explode.

'Please Shirley use your vibrator, let me hear it hum inside your cunt.' He begged.

It was making me feel really excited knowing how he felt and I must admit I wanted that vibrator inside me desperately. I put the phone onto loudspeaker so I could have both hands free.

'I'm holding my tits now Geoff and pushing them up and together just how you like it. I'm lying on the bed and now I'm making them shake from side to side. Do you like that?'

'Oh God.' Was all he said.

'I'm opening my legs for you and my hands are sliding down my tummy. Slowly, ever so slowly. My fingers reach between my legs and I can feel my lips and I'm pulling them apart for you. You can see inside me, you can see my pink wet flesh pouring with love juice that needs to be licked. Lick me Geoff, stick your tongue deep inside me and taste my juice. Run your tongue between my lips until it reaches my clitoris. I'm still holding my lips apart so you can really go to work on it. Lick me into a frenzy Geoff, lick it round and round and up and down. Take me to heights of ecstasy. But I want more. I want to feel your huge warm cock inside me, thrusting inside my cunt as far as it will reach and as far as I can take it. I'm switching it on. I can feel it touching my lips and I feel them parting as you slide inside me. Put your fist around your cock Geoff and feel my cunt lips suck you and squeeze you. Rub your shaft up and down and feel it deep inside my cunt, thrusting and ramming hard into me. Ramming so far up into me that you fill my cunt with your mighty cock. I can feel you Geoff, I can feel you deep inside me. So deeply that it is exquisite pain, that is the ultimate pleasure. I feel you swelling up inside me; I feel my cunt gripping your vibrating and pulsating cock. I can't control myself Geoff, I'm coming, oh God I'm coming. My whole body is shaking with an almighty orgasm and I hear you cry out in pleasure and I feel your hot semen shoot inside me in pulses of your orgasm.'

I lay there panting with the vibrator still pulsating inside me. I switched it off and sighed. Slowly I pulled it out and let it rest on the bed beside me; my cunt was glowing with pleasure. 'How are you Geoff?'

'Covered in semen.'

'Well I told you I would make it worthwhile you having a shower.'

Geoff was home by early evening and we had an early night and relived this morning's adventure.

A MAGIC COTTAGE

I arrived late afternoon in the little town that we called *our place*. A small romantic cottage tucked away from the rest of the world that Yvonne had discovered a few years ago. We had been coming back here every year, at least twice a year for the odd long weekend, or full week if we could spare the time. A place that was built in a more sedate era when urgent motor traffic wasn't a president and this slower pace was reflected by the narrow streets that years ago probably echoed with the clatter of hooves and the rumble of carts. I pulled into the pub car park opposite the cottage and went in for a drink and a bite to eat. Elizabeth, the lady who owned the cottage, had an agreement with the pub landlord and he allowed the residents, because of the lack of parking space, to use his car park. We had got to know Vince and Mave very well over the years and he kept an excellent pint of beer and Mave did a cracking Steak pie.

As I was about to enter, the smell of ale and home cooking swept through the open door and my mind went back to memories of the many happy visits Yvonne and I had there. And there across the road was Wren Cottage, our sanctuary from the cruel world. I felt a strange fluttery feeling in my stomach and felt my eyes beginning to feel tearful. I cleared my throat and told myself that things were different now, that I must get on with my life. But I couldn't help thinking about times past. Wren cottage looked inviting, but also daunting. This time I would be walking through that front door alone. Yvonne was cruelly and unexpectedly taken from me six months ago. I awoke one Sunday morning, but alas, she did not. She had gone peacefully in her sleep, she was just forty five.

I went into the pub and there was Vince as usual, newspaper on the bar, turned to the sports pages and picking his horses. He looked up as I entered. 'Hello Vince.' I said, feeling my voice waver.

'Ron. What can I say; we were absolutely devastated to hear about Yvonne.' Said Vince sympathetically.

'Oh, you've heard.' I said, relieved that I didn't have to tell him myself.

'Elizabeth called in and broke the news. Mave was really shaken.'

We spoke for a while about times past and Mave came through and gave her sympathy. I didn't stay long; just a quick drink to be polite then I went across to the cottage.

I stood outside just staring at it, we had many happy times there and I asked myself why was I here? I couldn't answer, it was just a feeling I had, an overwhelming compulsion that I must come here just one more time.

As I entered the cosy living room, a feeling of relaxation swept over me, it was exactly as we had left it. On the kitchen table, as usual was a bottle of wine and a small box of chocolates, a welcome gift from Elizabeth. Next to it a card, it read, "So sorry to hear of your sad loss. My heart goes out to you. Having lost my loved one, I know exactly how you must be feeling. I'm so pleased that you have come back to stay at Wren cottage, but equally, so sorry that Yvonne is no longer with you. Mere words cannot possibly convey my heartfelt condolences. I'm sure you've heard it many times but, time is a great healer. I shall call in over the next few days, but *if you need me please call me*. Elizabeth."

A very pleasant sentiment and I couldn't help but notice the emphasis she put on "if you need me please call me."

I settled myself in and unpacked. It didn't take long and after a light meal I sat myself down in the cosy living room and absorbed the atmosphere.

Various thoughts danced through my mind, why was I here, kept repeating itself, why was there such an overwhelming feeling that I should come alone? This place was almost our second home and I was here without Yvonne, and I thought about Elizabeth, I could not get her out of my mind. Why? I went through to the kitchen and got a beer from the fridge. As I took a drink I saw the card still on the table. I picked it up and read it again and those words beamed out at me again, "if you need me please call me." 'This is nonsense.' I said to myself. I returned to my easy chair and enjoyed my beer.

I sat with my thoughts and memories of times past, but all the time I was disturbed by the thoughts of Elizabeth. Apart from losing Yvonne, the circumstances with my job were changing. The company was, to use their expression, "consolidating its operations and was looking forward to a reappraised future." In common language it meant that the dinosaurs on the payroll were being offered a voluntary severance package. I have to admit that their offer was indeed attractive and I had decided to give it my consideration over the next few days. My thoughts however were disturbed once again by the image of Elizabeth in my mind. As a diversion I decided to switch on the T.V. In fact there was a documentary on later about astronomy, a subject that interested me greatly. I switched on. Nothing. Just a snowy screen. Damn, the thing isn't working. I switched it off, then on again, but no luck.

 "If you need me please call me." There it was again. 'O.K. you win Elizabeth, I'll phone.' I picked up the card and phoned the number.

 'Hello.'

 'Hello Elizabeth, its Ron.'

 'Ron, welcome back and again my heart felt condolences.'

 'Thank you. Look I'm sorry to disturb you at home, but I can't get the T.V. to work.'

Within fifteen minutes I saw her car pull into the pub car park. It had started to rain and Elizabeth ran across the road daintily in her high heels. I felt my heart flutter as she came towards me; it was as if destiny was propelling me along. I'm also ashamed to say I watched in amazement, as her large magnificent bust bounced up and down as she ran. I let her in and she left her umbrella by the door and adjusted her hair as she entered. 'I'm awfully sorry about this Elizabeth.'

'No problem, its me who should be apologising. Anyway, let's take a look at it.'

'Can I get you a coffee?'

'Yes, that would be nice, thank you.'

I went through to the kitchen leaving Elizabeth to deal with the T.V. As I prepared the coffee I could not help thinking about her and that image of her running across the road, her bust bouncing majestically was imprinted on my mind. Elizabeth was indeed a very attractive woman. She was only about five foot tall I would guess and as with a lot of short women, she had a very curvy figure. As I've mentioned a very ample and full bust, which I estimated to be forty two inch at least and given her short stature, it gives you some idea of her dimensions. She had a trim waist and very wide hips. Her face was pretty and round, with short dark hair that complemented her light hazel eyes. Dressed casually, but smartly with a dark maroon woollen top with a V neck and sleeves that extended midway down her forearms. Her hips were displayed magnificently by a pair of very tight black trousers. Not forgetting of course those high heeled black shoes that made her trot so seductively across the road.

As I re-entered the living room the T.V. was on with its familiar snowy screen. Elizabeth had the manual open on the seat of the armchair and leaning with a hand on each side arm I was treated to a spectacular view down her cleavage. And what a sight it was, forty two inches of succulent breasts encased in a very revealing bra. Very little was left to the imagination. I was about to offer her the coffee, but refrained as that would mean her standing up and I wanted to take in the view for as long as was possible. She turned the page and her breasts danced for me. She then came upon a possible solution and slapped the arm of the chair in triumph making her breasts wobble again. I stood in awe at the magnificent sight within her maroon top, with my mouth open and something stirring in my trousers.

'That's it I think.' She extolled and as she spoke she looked up and caught me looking down her top. Her eyes looked down momentarily and then looked into mine and she smiled knowingly with a glint in her eye. I gave a sort of embarrassed cough as I knew my voyeurism had been discovered. Feelings were stirring within me; I felt that destiny had bought me here, bought me here to Elizabeth. 'I'll put the coffee here.' I said rather weakly.

'Thank you. I think I know what the problem might be.'

She bent over the DVD and satellite receiver and reached behind the T.V. As she bent over her outline was too much to bear, those wide hips and beautiful round ass, well I felt like taking her there and then. Especially when she opened her legs to steady herself, I swear I could almost see the outline of her pussy lips through those tight trousers. She gyrated her hips and I got the impression she was doing it to tease me, and indeed she was, I could feel a bulge in my trousers and I tried to discreetly adjust myself for the sake of decency.

The television then burst into life.

'It just needed pushing in further.' She said as she stood up, pulling her top down and smoothing her hands over her breasts, with a very naughty twinkle in her eye. The hands caressing her breasts, was very erotic and it emphasised her nipples which were now very erect and showing through her top. I saw her eyes glance down at my shaft, which felt quite stiff and must almost certainly be showing. Elizabeth looked into my eyes and smiled. This was it. This is why I am here.

'Scart cable was loose.' She announced.

'Sorry.' I said, taken aback.

'The scart cable. I remember now, the people here last week had a computer game and asked if they could use it with the T.V. They obviously removed the cable and didn't fit it back properly.'

'I see.'

'Probably a bit stiff.' She said seductively and simultaneously glancing down at my loins.

We stared in silence at each other for a few moments. I knew in my mind that it was my place to make a move. The signals were there, I had to take the initiative now or the moment would be lost forever. I took her forearms, pulling her towards me, my hands sliding down to meet hers. As we held hands our eyes met and said everything. I wanted Elizabeth;

I wanted her both spiritually and physically. We fell into each others arms and I felt her heaving bosom against me, she looked into my eyes and we kissed. We kissed so longingly and as we did so my mind went over the image of that plunging cleavage and those huge breasts hanging there. Those round hips and her round backside that was so inviting, as she bent over with her legs apart. An image that said, 'take me.'

The fire was up and the passion was at boiling point. As we kissed my hand found her breast, it felt exactly as I'd imagined, large, full and firm. I felt her hands slide down my back and clutch my buttocks, grasping and massaging them just as I was doing the same to her huge breast. Our breathing was heavy and our kissing becoming more passionate and exciting. I felt her hand slide around my hips until it found my very erect and throbbing shaft. Her hand gently followed its length and contours and she moaned gently as she gauged its size. I let my hands slide to her waist and under her top. I lifted it up and she raised her arms to let it slip over her head. I stepped back and stood with my mouth open gaping at her bosom barely encased in a delicate white lacy bra, which seemed very flimsy for the task of containing those huge breasts. She reached round and unclipped her bra. It almost seemed as though it wanted to shoot off on its own, but Elizabeth taunted me as she peeled the straps from her shoulders and slowly let it slide away to reveal a sight that mere words are incapable of describing. She cast her bra aside like unwanted litter and as she did so her breasts swayed from side to side, I was in awe at such a majestic sight. Elizabeth then unzipped her trousers and slowly pushed them down her thighs, leaning forward so her breasts dangled before me, as she stepped out of her trousers they gently waved from side to side. She breathed in slowly, sticking out her chest and slowly caressed her breasts, supporting them gently in her hands. They were beautiful, so large and so firm and so natural. Her nipples were large and erect and her areola was a good three inches across, dark pink with a perimeter of small dark nodules. She stood there wearing only her delicate pink knickers.

It was now my move; I unbuttoned my shirt and cast it aside, quickly followed by my trousers, shoes, socks and shorts. I stood naked before her and she licked her lips as she inspected me, her eyes coming to rest on my aching shaft. Elizabeth pushed down her knickers giving me another display of her magnificent breasts. What a perfect naked figure she had, large firm breasts and wide round hips. I was at bursting point. I took my shaft in my hand and let it slowly slide along its length. Elizabeth gasped gently. I sensed that we were both ready for hot sex.

Elizabeth took the initiative and pushed me onto the settee
   'Sit.' She commanded.
   I willingly obeyed. Then she straddled me, reaching down to take my shaft and slowly lowering herself onto it, guiding my throbbing cock between her glistening wet labial lips. Once safely inside, she slid down my length. The feeling of it entering her body was unbelievable; it was so warm and moist. The inside of her cunt felt like the centre of the universe. I felt my cock sink inside her and she moaned with sheer intimate pleasure. Elizabeth then leaned forward and placed her hands on the back of the settee and slid her hips back and forward, rubbing her clitoris against my pelvic bone. She did it so slowly and purposely, I could feel my shaft swaying with the motion inside her. Her strokes were gauged perfectly for maximum stimulation. Her cunt gripped my shaft and at times it almost seemed that she would rip it off, but she knew the score and she rode me like an expert. She was in complete control, her hands on the back of the settee and her knees either side of me, I was in her power. Her rhythm got faster and faster, her face an expression of consuming ecstasy and as she fucked me I was able to watch her tits bouncing about, they went up and down and banged together in wild indulgence, occasionally slapping my face. It was a wonderful sight and that combined with my shaft deeply inside her, the effect was euphoria, pure euphoria. Her clitoris dug deeply into me with every thrust, her eyes glazed and her face contorted with the agony of supreme pleasure. Faster and faster she went, thrusting harder and harder, her tits bouncing into a blur. Her breathing became deeper then stopped momentarily as she screamed out in an explosive orgasm. Her cunt seemed almost to suck me inside her and I could feel the convulsions grip me. Slowly her orgasm began to level out and her gyrating hips and her bouncing breasts started to settle down. She sighed the sigh of someone fulfilled. 'My turn now.' I said.

'How do you want to take me?' She sighed submissively as she stood up, her cunt giving my shaft one last suck.

I took all the cushions off the furniture and placed them in two piles on the floor. I couldn't get the image of her bending over the T.V. out of my mind, so I was now going to live out my fantasy. 'Kneel down.' I commanded. She knew what I had in mind and kneeled on the pile of cushions with her legs apart. I could see her glowing cunt and her lips were open and waiting for me. I didn't intend keeping them waiting long. I fell to my knees behind her and guided my throbbing cock between her lips. They parted as I entered her and Elizabeth gave a gentle moan. I positioned my knees and took hold of those wonderful wide hips and thrust my shaft into her tight little cunt. Elizabeth screamed as my cock stabbed deeply inside her. It was beautiful, too beautiful and I just wanted to fuck her hard, and I did so, I rammed my shaft inside her like a demon. She cried out with pleasure as I thrust harder and harder, my shaft reaching right into her cunt. Gripping her hips, I pulled her hard onto me with every thrust. All too soon the ecstasy was too much for me and I felt a volcanic eruption building within me that had to be vented. I came in a welter of pleasure and filled her eager little cunt with a pulsating torrent of hot semen.

We spent the afternoon in each others arms and the evening, a romantic candle lit supper and planning a happy future.

TABLE TOP SALE

It was a beautiful sunny Sunday morning in early April and the sunlight cascaded through the blossom laden trees. I heard the birds merrily singing and breathed in the sweet smell of spring. In some ways I considered myself an extremely fortunate woman, I lived in this beautiful chocolate box cottage, in a beautiful little village, in a rural part of England where, it seemed that time had stood still. A small river flowed past the bottom of my manicured garden and continued through the village, the main street of which crossed it by means of an eighteenth century stone bridge. A scene of classical tranquillity and beauty, typical of a Turner or Constable painting you might say.

I had lived here all my married life and John and I were happy and content and produced a beautiful daughter, who is now living in America with her husband and baby daughter. Alas John was taken from me fifteen years ago and I have had a solitary widow's life since. Friends have said that I should remarry, that I was only fifty, which was still young these days. I am very grateful for their concern and support, but the fact remains that I am fifty and all eligible men of similar age are married. Plus life in the village, although pleasant, does not contain a huge pool of available manhood. A few years ago I did have a girl's night out in town as a sort of match making evening, but nothing really came of it, in fact it was an embarrassing disaster that I feel uncomfortable talking about. So since then I have accepted my lot and was grateful for the short but happy marriage with John and decided I would just live my life and go with the flow of village life.

The bedside clock said seven thirty, time to get moving. Today a table top sale had been organised in the village hall and I had volunteered to help out, making coffee and sandwiches and such like. I slid out of bed, yawned and stretched. As I did so I caught sight of myself in the mirror standing in my red nightie with a little bear on the front. My hair was a little tousled, but nothing a quick flick with a comb would not put right. I kept it short and colored chestnut brown with a gold tinge. It was in reasonable condition, parted in the middle and just covered my ears. A small fringe completed the simple style. I had been told that I had a very girlish face with cute dimples when I smiled and a nose that wrinkled slightly and looked angelic when I laughed. I had never been sure what they meant by that last description, but I was grateful for the complements. So for a fifty year old my face and hair were fine.

My body however posed another problem, if indeed problem was the correct word and I stood there looking at it, enrobed in my teddy bear nightie. All my adult life I had what was considered a full figure. What that meant in reality was that I was just under the point of being described as obese, but having larger than average breasts. When we were first married they measured a very ample forty two inches with double D cups and I remember with fond memories the effect that they had on John, but alas those days are no more. However since I was about forty a metabolic change seemed to be taking place and my breasts seemed to get larger. I'm assured that this is not unusual in middle aged women, but in most women their bodies expand in all directions. In my case the rest of my body stayed more or less the same; it was just my breasts that were running away with over development. In one respect it was quite disturbing and I had even sought advice on surgical reduction but was advised against it. To help tone down my appearance I had taken to wearing loose fitting clothing, such as kaftan styles, which were not unlike my nighties in design. They at least made my body look in proportion, in other words fat all over. It seemed, thankfully, over the past few years their enlargement seemed to have stopped and they have come to a thankful halt at fifty eight inches. The cup size however has gone off the scale and I have to have my brassieres specially made. Very expensive, but they do have the quality of visually reducing the size of my breasts, so well worth it.

I stood looking in the mirror and sighed and lifted my nightie over my head throwing it casually onto the bed. There it was, the body, in all its glory, predominated by huge breasts. I have to admit that, although they were large, they were also very firm, so in that respect nature had been kind to me, it would have looked obscene if they had just drooped around my waist. They stuck out from my chest at least twelve inches without hardly any sag and when I moved they just bobbed alluringly. It was almost as if they had implants, but these were real. I wonder if any man will ever enjoy them I thought to myself, my hands holding them up from underneath. The areola, the colored discs around my nipples were very dark, almost as dark as someone who has just had a baby and were nearly four inches across.

As I caressed my breasts my nipples were becoming very erect and I felt a wanton tingle of excitement running through my body. I took my nipples between my thumbs and forefingers and tweaked them gently making them even firmer. It was very pleasant. With both hands I lifted my right breast to my mouth and kissed my nipple. I was beginning to feel very aroused and I wanted to go further and took my nipple in my mouth, sucking it gently and flicking it with my tongue then sucking it again. It took me back to the time when John used to do this to me and I found it very stimulating. I had little experience of men before John and none afterwards so I found it difficult to know what was normal in terms of sexual practices. Plus being bought up in a small community where sex was never discussed in polite conversation I had no idea what other women accepted as their *norm*. Even what I was doing now, this self adoration I felt somewhat guilty about, but then I thought why not, no one can see me and it is giving me sexual pleasure, sexual pleasure that I am unlikely to get from anywhere else. As I continued to fondle my breast with my hands and suck my ever hardening nipple I lifted my eyes and saw my image in the mirror. My initial feeling of depravity rapidly gave way to a sense of wonder lust and the fact I could see myself giving myself pleasure gave it a totally new and wonderful dimension. I let my enormous breast fall and it fell back into place with a couple of gentle wobbles. I leaned forward a little so my giant orbs dangled slightly and I let them shake from side to side. My initial self consciousness was turning into pride. I was in the privacy of my bedroom and a sexual adventure was unfolding before me, a fantasy that I could indulge in without caring about what anyone thought. My huge waving breasts still dangled before me. I stood up straight and stuck my chest out. What a show off I thought. I put my hands on the top of my chest and slowly let them follow the contours of my breasts; it was indeed a sensual sight to see. My tiny hands following every curve, sliding underneath and lifting them high and pushing them together, making a vast valley of cleavage. Pulling them apart them pushing them together and upwards. My arms stretched out so I could reach around to the front of them, once again taking my nipples between thumb and forefinger and teasing them to greater erection. I pushed them up to my mouth and kissed and sucked each nipple in turn. I was becoming very excited, my mind taken over by this feeling of primitive lust, a lust that was slowly building to a crescendo of ultimate pleasure.

I let them fall and I gasped with pleasure I shook my shoulders so my breasts shook violently, it was an amazing sight to see, fifty eight inches of unfettered breasts shaking with sexual energy. Again I let my hands flow down from my chest and followed my contours. I felt I needed more, I needed satisfaction and fulfilment. My hands flowed over my breasts to my tummy, I could hear my heart beating and my breathing was heavy. My hands travelled further, on down to my lower abdomen, here my left hand travelled on alone and I watched it all in the mirror. I parted my legs slightly as my fingers travelled over my pubic mound and gently my middle finger slid gently between my legs. I gasped once more as my finger parted my moist lips. It travelled further and my vulva was soaked with love juice as my finger went further between my wet and eager lips. I was in a state of complete abandonment and all I craved for was sexual fulfilment, I needed it now and I was going to get it. I explored my lips and found my clitoris, the moment my finger gently touched it I screamed out with pleasure. This was the ultimate pleasure and as I stood watching myself in the mirror it seemed to make it more exciting. I held open my lips with the first two fingers of the other hand, this gave me more intimate access to my clitoris, plus it gave me a better view in the mirror. I fingered myself slowly at first gathering speed as the pleasure increased. As I did so my enormous breasts were responding by bouncing and shaking uncontrollably. It was an incredible sight watching myself being given the ultimate pleasure and my breasts out of control. On and on I went, stimulating my clitoris further and further until I felt myself on the brink of ecstasy and with one gentle stroke I screamed out with sheer undiluted climax. It was like an explosion of fantastic and indescribable pleasure. I continued to finger myself as my orgasm went on and on. Eventually it levelled out and I slowly began to regain control. There I stood exhausted but happy and more importantly I felt a great feeling of liberation. I could have cheerfully gone back to bed and slept until lunch time, but I had promised to help out in the village hall so a revitalising shower was called for.

The table top sale seemed to go well and the traders were now starting to pack up. I was also about to start clearing up the kitchen. As I did so my thoughts kept going back to earlier this morning and my performance in front of the mirror. It was wantonly wicked and I should have felt ashamed of myself, but then why I thought, probably everyone does it, but it's not the sort of thing you talk about.

'Anymore coffee left?' Came a voice from the serving hatch to the hall.

I turned and it was a rather handsome and distinguished looking man of about thirty five. I must admit I was attracted to him and this plus my sexual daydreaming, well, I could feel my face flush slightly, almost as if I felt he knew what I had been thinking about. I served him his coffee and he smiled a smile that made me melt.

'Thank you very much.'

'Did you enjoy the sale?' I asked, clumsily trying to make conversation.

'Yes, very good. Picked up an old video I haven't seen for years.

My mouth and brain dried as I tried desperately to think of something to keep a conversation going. I felt an unexplainable feeling towards this man and although he seemed fifteen years my junior, I wanted to get to know more about him. As he drank his coffee I could see him eyeing up my bust.

'Anymore sugar Joan?' shouted Sue.

'Should be some in the top cupboard.' I replied.

'Well see you again sometime.' Said the man as he finished his coffee.

'Yes, please come again.' I said my words fading into the air as he disappeared through the door probably never to be seen again.

After lunch I pottered about in the front garden just tidying up and thinking about the events of the day and the man at the sale. It was a lovely afternoon, the sun was shining and a fresh breeze was still gently blowing.

'Hello again.' Said a voice.

I turned and it was the man from the sale.

'Hello again.' I replied, pleasantly surprised.

'Its Joan isn't it?'

'Yes, but how do...'

'The woman in the kitchen, asked you for the sugar.'

I was flattered that he remembered my name.

'I've seen you around the village a few times as I've driven through and I saw you in your garden as I drove past just now, so I walked back to say hello and thank you again for the coffee.'

I was beginning to feel more flattered and I felt my face flush again. I felt I must do something as he had made the first move. 'I was about to have some tea, would you care to join me.' I ventured, 'or coffee if you would prefer.'

'Tea would be fine, thank you. Oh, I'm Roger.' He said offering his hand.

'Nice to meet you.' I said removing my gardening glove and taking his hand.

He held my hand and we looked into each others eyes. Now I had heard about love at first sight and I was not sure if it existed, but if it did I think this was it.

We sat on the settee and had tea and talked about this and that and it transpired that Roger had also been widowed and was living alone. There was a silence, a silence that spoke a thousand words, a silence of feelings being exchanged. Roger turned to me and took my chin gently in his hands, lifting my face to his and his lips to mine. We kissed gently and stared at each other, our eyes had the fire of raw passion that needed to be satisfied. We kissed again, this time with great urgency, holding each other tightly and Rogers tongue finding mine. I could feel the sexual energy within his body and I wanted it. He was breathing heavily as he kissed me and I could feel his hand beginning to wander. It found and caressed my breast and I felt his fingers toying with my erect nipple. I could feel his body shaking, shaking with electric hot desire. His hand slid down my side, over my hips and down my thigh. It stopped at my hem and I felt his fingers creep under my dress and travel up my stocking covered thigh. Slowly it went down again and he transferred his hand to my other thigh, the inside of my other thigh. His fingers felt the resistance of my other leg, so I slowly and gently opened them. As he kissed me I felt him sigh and his hand continued its journey upwards between my thighs, those two converging highways that led to the epitome of ecstasy. I felt his fingers on the bare flesh above my stocking tops and opening my legs further I gasped as they reached my pussy and I could feel that my knickers were soaked with my love juice. He lovingly caressed my hot lips through my wet knickers. I gently pushed his hand away and stood up, he looked at me longingly. I took his hand and led him up to my bed.

I did not stand on ceremony, this morning I was liberated; I was going to be liberated again. I was wearing a loose dress and I unzipped the back and let it fall to the floor. Roger gasped at what he saw and realised that I didn't fill all of the dress, just the top half. I unclipped my bra and let the straps slide from my shoulders and my breasts stuck out twelve inches towards him. Sliding my fingers into my wet panties I slid them down my thighs until gravity made them complete their journey. I put my leg on the bed and slid down my stocking. Like the whore I felt, I opened my legs so he could see the wet lips of my pussy. I repeated the operation with my other stocking, adjusting my stance so again he had full view of my womanhood. There I was naked and free. Roger stood entranced at the sight. I shook my breasts for him and this seemed to do the trick, he immediately undressed and we stood naked facing each other. I had not seen many men intimately, but I have to say that Roger seemed to be very well endowed. His penis was hugely erect and must have been at least eight inches long and his purple bulbous end was particularly striking, the rim of which stood a good quarter of an inch proud of his shaft. I looked at it longingly imagining it inside me, that bulbous rim stimulating the inside of my womanhood. But I knew that I didn't have to imagine for long, because I knew it would soon be happening for real.

Roger walked towards me and took my breasts in his hands. I closed my eyes and sighed at the pleasure of it all. He fondled and caressed them and fell to his knees and rubbed his face between them, sucking, licking and biting me desperately. Passion was burning between both of us and we could feel it. He started to kiss my tummy and continued lower and lower until he reached my pubic mound. He sat me on the bed and still kneeling he pulled my knees apart; it gave me a magical thrill knowing that he could see me so intimately and Roger gasped at the sight. He kissed my knee and slowly kissed the inside of my thigh, getting higher and higher. He lifted my legs over his shoulder and I lay back on the bed, locking my feet around his neck. I was in a state of ecstasy and I wanted him to go faster. Higher and higher he went and I moaned loudly as he kissed my vulva. I could feel my lips parting and it was an almost automatic and uncontrollable urge that made me reach down with my fingers and open them wider for him. Roger gasped as my clitoris was exposed for his pleasure. He wasted no time and got to work on it with his tongue immediately. He licked me so expertly and erotically, it was unbelievably beautiful and before long I could feel the pleasure building up within my body. He timed his strokes so perfectly and I felt I was just one lick away from utopia; I just wanted that one more stroke to take me to heaven. My body ached for it and then it came over me, it was all consuming I was powerless in a wave of ultimate pleasure. It was the best ever, it seemed to go on forever, and it was almost frightening, almost as if it was not going to stop. I pushed Rogers head because I thought I was stuck in perpetual orgasm. Roger just gripped my thighs harder, holding me down to the bed and the orgasm just went on higher to greater ecstasy. I screamed and cried, I was out of control consumed with orgasmic euphoria. Eventually it levelled out and I gripped Rogers head almost as if I was trying to pull him inside me, I wanted more. Eventually it did subside and I was still crying.

Gently but firmly Roger told me to turn over and kneel on the edge of the bed and I willingly obeyed and kneeled on all fours with my legs open ready to receive him. Also for the second time today I could see myself naked in the mirror and my breasts were hanging and almost touching the bed. I could see Roger standing behind me, he had his huge shaft in his hand and he was guiding it to its destination. I felt his bulbous end enter me, pushing my lips apart. Not only could I feel it but I could see it in the mirror. His penis entered me and I saw Roger take hold of my hips, as he pulled me back onto himself and I felt his mighty shaft slide deeply into me. It was wonderful, it was so large I could feel it stretching me and reaching the very top of my vagina, I could feel that huge bulbous end rubbing my inside, stimulating me. On and on he thrust and I watched his shaft sliding in and out, glistening with my love juice and every stroke, every thrust getting harder and more urgent. Faster and faster he went, gripping my hips, pulling me hard onto his shaft, my breasts shaking with his motion and banging together. Eventually with a cry like thunder I felt Roger come inside me, my vagina seemingly gripping and sucking his penis, sucking out his semen as it pumped inside me. Our lust was sated and Roger stood, still gripping my hips, his erection still deep inside me. Finally, as lovers do we fell asleep together completely satisfied. That afternoon was the start of a deep and loving relationship and a new life for us both.

THE MAN ON THE HORSE

It was five o'clock; I dropped the folder into the cabinet and slid it shut with an air of relief. The day was finally over, I covered the computer, picked up my bag and grabbed my coat, the rest of the office were similarly following suit.

'Doing anything special this weekend Kate'? Enquired Linda.

I gave a knowing smile. 'Going to the coast with Gareth'.

'Oh it's getting serious. It will be wedding bells soon'

'Well we'll see'. I said trying to side step any further conversation on the subject. It was true Gareth and I were getting very close but I had previously had a bad encounter of the marriage kind and I wanted to be sure it wouldn't happen again. It had also been confirmed that I was pregnant and I needed to discuss the matter with Gareth.

My suitcase was already in the car and it was a simple matter of driving to our favourite hotel for the rendezvous. I drove off and the smog of the days toil blew away with the fresh spring air coming through the car window. I was looking forward to the weekend. We had been to this particular hotel a number of times now, it was quiet and secluded, as was the town, which had a small promenade that was west facing and sheltered by mountains behind. I had decided to take an alternative route as recommended by Gareth. True it was slightly longer but the picturesque countryside more than made up for the few extra miles.

The sun was shining from an almost cloudless clear blue sky, the birds were singing and all was well with the world. Unusually for me, I put the radio on and listened to some very soothing classical music. I had the volume very low so it was background music that complemented the sounds of the countryside. All was wonderful and I was in good spirits. The sun was getting lower in the sky now and the fields and hedgerows took on a magical eventide appearance, it was far from dusk and I knew I would be with Gareth long before sunset so we could have one of our romantic walks along the promenade before dinner.

Unfortunately with my day dreaming I took a wrong turning at a crossroads. 'No matter' I thought, just continue on until I find a turning and retrace my steps. I hoped it would not be long, as the road was deteriorating and not even surfaced in places with a frightening number of potholes which shook the car violently. The weather too had suddenly taken a turn for the worse and the sky was filled with threatening storm clouds. The radio started to crackle and the signal began to fade. I tried tuning to another station but to no avail. It started to rain and very quickly it became torrential. The radio failed completely to a monotone hiss. Probably due to this strange weather I thought. Thankfully, through the lashing rain I saw a lane ahead in which I could turn around. Then to my horror, from nowhere a young girl was standing in the middle of the road. I slammed on the brakes and swerved but I new in my mind I would hit her. The car slid on the muddy surface and hit a tree at the end of the lane. Fortunately I had my seat belt on but I was badly shaken and temporarily disorientated. I could not understand why the car lost control. I was not going fast and although the road surface, such as it was, was wet, the brakes seemed to have no effect whatsoever.

'The child' I suddenly blurted out, 'oh my God I must have killed her'.

I leapt out of the car, my head feeling like it was going to burst. It was like one of those recurring nightmares that you get, when you know you have killed someone and you are a fugitive. Then you wake up and all is well. But I knew I would not wake up and all was far from well. I staggered though mud and rain to see if I could help the child, if by some miracle she was still alive.

To my utter disbelief, there she was, still standing in the middle of the road. She had a strange expression on her face; she was looking towards me, but through me. She stood in the pouring rain the wind blowing her soaking locks. I felt a ghostly, shivering tingle run up my arms.

'Are you alright'? I called out, but she just wiped a lock of curly hair from her brow and did not answer. A feeling of slight relief was coming over me, at least she was still alive, but what injuries had she sustained. What also puzzled me was the way she was dressed. She had long blond hair that was now in sodden ringlets. A white pinafore over a dark dress of seemingly very thick material that came down to below her knees. She had thick dark stockings and black shoes with large buckles. My fascination with her dress was cut short by a strange sound approaching from behind.

I turned and to my horror coming up the road, straight for us was a huge carriage being driven at great speed, pulled by four black horses. It was driven by a demented spectral figure dressed in a black caped coat and wide brimmed hat that hid his face. His bony, almost skeletal hand waved a whip, with which he was pushing the snorting and protesting beasts to their utmost effort. I half dived and half slipped as I tried to pull the child out of its path. But to my horror my arms seemed to go through her and I fell headlong into a muddy pool. I quickly rolled over as the pounding hooves and wheels thundered past my head.

'The girl' I shouted 'the carriage will hit the girl'.

I quickly staggered to my feet and ran into the road. There was nothing. No coach. No child. Absolutely nothing. No sound other than the pattering of the rain. I could not believe what I had just witnessed, nor could I explain it. I returned to my unroadworthy car for my mobile, to summon help and tell Gareth of my disaster. I sat in the car dripping wet and found my phone.

'No signal, wonderful'.

Nothing for it, I thought as I emerged into the rain once more, I shall have to walk to find a telephone to get help and also report the maniac in the coach to the police. I looked down the lane and noticed a cottage. There was a light in the window so I thought I would try there first. It was now getting dark and the faint light of the cottage was very comforting. It was only a hundred yards away and as I walked towards it my mind mused over the puzzling events. What was the mysterious girl doing in the road? Maybe she lived at the cottage. Why was she wearing such strange clothes, clothes I had seen people wearing in period dramas set in the late nineteenth century. And also the great coach, which was from the same era. What was the story behind that? As I walked I tried to work it out but couldn't. There was something else. How could the weather change so suddenly and dramatically? I pondered the problem, and then another problem presented itself. I had been walking towards the cottage for quiet a few minutes now and I had not got any closer, and yet my car appeared to be about a quarter of a mile away as I looked back. I stood there not knowing what to do next, I felt very lost and very alone and very scared. All sorts of thoughts raced through my mind, none of which made much sense. I closed my eyes in the feeble hope that when I opened them all would be normal. I felt the rain on my face as I stood there thinking. When I opened them I froze with fear, I was face to face with a towering black horse upon which sat a rider draped in oilskins. In terror I looked up, but his face was hidden in the shadow of his hat. I could take no more, my head was still pounding from the crash, my thoughts were becoming swirling mists of confusion and I seemed to lose consciousness and just collapsed in the mud.

I awoke to what seemed to be early morning. I was feeling very weak and fragile and my head still felt weird, I'm afraid I cannot explain myself any clearer than that. I felt a sort of feeling of detachment. As I lay there I could hear the birds singing and sunlight cascaded into the room through an open window made of small leaded panels, a breeze gently moving the crude curtains. There was the sound of wood being chopped. It took a few moments to come to full consciousness. My mind went over the night before. The crash, the mysterious child, the spectral carriage and the mysterious man on the horse. I pushed back the blanket away and got out of bed, which was comfortable but crudely made, almost home made. The rustic nature of the bed was complemented by the rustic nature of my nightdress. This is not mine I thought and where are my clothes? What time is it? My watch was gone and there were no clocks in the room. A candle was burning on the top of a wooden chest in the corner of the room and there were several other, as yet unused candles here and there and there was a marked absence of electric lights or even anything electric. It struck me that if the owner was so techno phobic it was probably very likely that there was no phone either.

I went to the window and looked out. There was a man, a very good looking man chopping wood. He was stripped to the waist and had long hair tied back with a black ribbon. His body was illuminated and highlighted by the sunshine beyond him, which made his body glow. Although it was a chill morning the sun caught the drops of sweat that fell at every swing of his mighty axe, illuminating them like tiny sparkling beads. There was a light ground mist amongst the trees that one sees at this hour that is ephemeral and dissolves away in the rising morning sun. The sun beams played through the trees and with every mighty effort, the man's breath could be seen in clouds on the cold morning air. I watched this magnificent specimen almost forgetting about the strange events of yesterday. Was he the mysterious man on the horse? Was it he that removed my clothes and put me to bed. My mind raced with the thoughts of what else he had done to me and indeed may do to me in the future. I clutched my throat and felt the smoothness of the material of my nightdress half in fear and half in fascination of this romantic figure chopping wood.

I was startled by the door suddenly opening and there stood a pleasant young woman of a similar age to me dressed in a long black skirt, full frilly white blouse and a small white apron. She had in her hands a simple wooden tray with two wooden bowls, the larger containing what looked like a vegetable broth and the smaller one milk.

'Did you sleep well my dear'? She enquired. 'I've bought you something to eat'.

'Oh yes, thank you,' was all I was able to say.

'Well, now you are up perhaps you would like to join Jed and me at the kitchen table'.

With that I followed her through the door. The kitchen had the same rustic style as the bedroom and I could see that she did all her cooking over an open fire. The situation had a definite weird feel about it. We sat at the table and immediately the door opened and in walked the Adonis of the wood pile.

'You're awake then lassie' he boomed.

'Yes, and I'd like to thank you and your wife for putting me up'. I said humbly.

'Ha ha, he ain't my husband he be my brother' said the woman.

'Oh' I said, still trying to puzzle out this situation.

'Martha won't let me wed until she finds a husband. Doesn't want to be left without a man of sorts'.

'My name is Kate' I said holding the milk bowl to my lips.

'Oh yes and where you be from Kate?' asked Jed.

'Well I was driving from...'

'Driving'? Interrupted Martha. 'Women don't drive'.

'Steady on Martha, Lady Margaret used to drive'. He said as he joined us at the table.

'Yes but only around the estate Jed'.

'Well where's your carriage then Kate?'

Well I have a car if that is what you mean.

'What is a car'? Asked Martha with a genuine ignorance that worried me.

'You know Martha one of those mechanical carriages that his Lordship used to talk about'.

My heart was beginning to sink. This was either some elaborate practical joke or these people where simpletons who had turned their back on the modern world and gone back to nature. There was also the impossible option that somehow I was the outsider. Something else I had noticed since waking was the silence. True there was the sound of Jed's chopping and the birds and other country sounds, but there were no sounds of the distant hum of traffic, or even aircraft. And in the clear blue sky there was no evidence of any vapour trails. I was beginning to fear that the impossible was becoming frighteningly possible. There were no newspapers about either, because it crossed my mind that there may be some mention of me being missing and I needed to know the date without having to ask. It seemed however, that, that was my only option.

'What's the date'? I enquired as casually as possible.

'Why I believe it's the fifth of May' replied Martha.

'And the year'? I said casually.

They both looked at each other.

'1890 of course'. Replied Jed tersely.

I tried to hide my feelings, but at that news I fell to a new level of depression. I suddenly thought about my wrecked car. We had finished our meal and I suggested a walk hoping that the only lifeline to reality was still there. Jed offered to accompany me and I welcomed this as I wanted to get him on his own and perhaps somehow explain my fears.

It was a beautiful day; the air was clean and fresh as we walked along the lane to the road.

'This is where I found you' said Jed halting in his tracks.

The blurry events of last night were coming back to me. The man on the horse was Jed. We reached the main road and a fresh wave of depression came over me. The car had gone. I thought maybe it had been towed away by the police but the mud was still soft from the previous night's rain and there were no tracks. There had never been a car there and I felt strangely empty inside.

'What is it lass'. Said Jed, sensing my mood.

I could take no more and just fell into his arms crying. He held me firmly and his hand stroked my hair. I gripped him tightly. He was now the only strand of what now passed as reality and I cried and I cried and I cried.

Jed comforted me and I pulled myself together with a brave sniff and a deep breath. It was obvious that no amount of tears was going to help my situation. We walked on and I asked Jed about his life. He told me how he used to be a game keeper at the big house beyond his cottage and he would take me to see it. We set off, walking along lanes and through fields, Jed acknowledging his contemporaries as they passed.

'Nearly there' he said as we arrived at the top of the field. 'There it is'. He said with remorse in his voice and the hint of a tear in his eye. 'The Manor'.

It was a shell, a ruined shell that had obviously been ravaged by fire.

You could see by what was left that in its day it would have been a very large and grand place.

'It's been like that some five years now'.

'And you used to work there'?

'Aye that I did, gamekeeper, as was my father before me, and Martha worked as scullery maid.

'So what happened'?

'Well some say there was a curse on the family. Poor Sir Hector. Spent his final years in black remorse'.

Jed was obviously very emotional about the subject and I let him tell his story in his own time.

'It was all the fault of Edward his wastrel of a son. He squandered his money on gambling and stole the family treasures to pay his creditors. Lady Margaret, his mother had died suddenly and it devastated the family, in fact the whole village. Except Edward of course who ransacked the house while the family and staff were at the funeral. Sir Hector was full of rage and grief and stormed around the house inspecting the deflowered walls that once contained priceless paintings'.

'That is terrible. How can anyone steel from their own family when they are in the depths of grief. And, while everyone was at the funeral, which is even more despicable'.

'Not everyone was at the funeral. There was a daughter, Louise, twelve years old and the apple of Sir Hectors' eye. Since the actions of his son she was to be the heir to the estate. Except the hand of tragedy took over'.

'What happened'? I said, almost fearful of hearing the answer.

'Louise stayed at our cottage with Martha until the funeral was over. She was unaware of her elder brothers gambling and what he was doing to the family fortune. In the evening she walked back to the Manor with Martha and the weather suddenly turned foul. Sir Hector was in a red rage and knew that his son was taking the treasures to the coast so he had the carriage made ready with four horses and he gave chase'.

'Louise being a highly strung girl was making light of the weather and was jumping in the puddles in the road, when suddenly Sir Hector rounded the bend in his carriage and in the blinding rain and blinding rage didn't see his daughter and ran over her breaking her poor little body. That was five years ago last night'.

I suddenly felt quite sick. I had seen that apparition last night. Jed continued.

'Sir Hector never recovered. All he loved had been taken from him. He dismissed all the staff and started fires throughout the Manor. He sat down in his library and took a fatal dose of his medication and waited to be reunited with his Lady Margaret and beloved Louise'.

In silence we returned to the cottage. In the days to come I began to accept the inevitable, at least in part. I knew I had had a car accident and somehow that had affected me, and I hoped that in time all would clarify itself and I would see my world again.

I became very close to Jed and in time we became lovers and I took him to my bed. It was a beautiful evening, Jed had been chopping wood and Martha was visiting friends, we had the place to ourselves. He entered with an armful of logs and just stood and stared at me from the doorway. I knew I wanted him and he sensed my longing. He cast aside his logs and took me in his arms, his manly aroma intoxicated me and I wanted his body, I wanted to be made love to. He scooped me up in his arms and carried me through to the bedroom where he gently lay me down. I was wearing only my nightdress and as I lay on the bed I wriggled out of it. Jed stood there looking at my naked body. My nipples were erect and I could feel the tingle within my vagina. I wanted his manhood thrusting inside me. Jed took off his boots, then his shirt to reveal his suntanned manly chest. He was wiry without an ounce of fat. His muscles like whipcord. He unclipped his strap and his trousers fell to the floor. His shaft was hard and throbbing, his huge purple bulbous end looked close to bursting. I wanted it in me; I wanted to feel the ripple of that huge cock inside my cunt rubbing my G-spot to ecstasy. He stood panting at the end of the bed, I raised my knees and opened my legs, and he gasped at the sight of my wet glistening lips. I slowly moved my hands down and with my fingers I pulled open my lips so Jed could see the promise of pleasure that was waiting within me. I put my hands behind my knees to pull my legs back and to hold them open wider. Jed could contain himself no longer, he kneeled between my thighs and I could feel his massive penis entering me. He lifted my buttocks to his level and his huge shaft slid inside me. I could feel the rim of his cock rasping the inside of my cunt. It was unbelievable, I had never taken a cock as big as this before and it was wonderful. Onwards he thrust, ramming his huge penis deeply inside me. He held my hips and forced me down onto his cock. It hurt slightly, but it was a pain of intense pleasure. Eventually I could feel an orgasm building and Jed was coming at the same time. We simultaneously screamed with pleasure as I climaxed, my cunt sucking his pulsating cock which throbbed as his hot semen shot inside me and burst out of me with every thrust. Eventually the pleasure died down and we held each other in silent rapture.

Time passed by and Jed had offered his hand in marriage and I willingly accepted. Arrangements were made and we were to be married in a month. Sir Hector had made a small provision for both Jed and Martha in his will and the cottage belonged to them. Sir Hector had also left them with a respectable annuity. A little later Martha had been offered marriage by the local innkeeper which she graciously accepted. Life was turning out splendidly I thought.

The big day arrived and we were married. It was a double marriage and Martha moved into the local inn to be the landlady and Jed and I had the cottage to ourselves. Many spring mornings I awoke to the sound of Jed chopping wood, the incoming sun illuminating his virile body. To make our happiness complete before our first year was out I found I was with child.

A few weeks later I lay awake on a spring evening, feeling disturbed and uneasy, it was the fourth of May. It was exactly a year since my arrival. And, as that fateful night, it was raining. I was beginning to drift into slumber when I heard a loud crash. Jed did not disturb. Something possessed me, I had to go and look. I went out in the pouring rain with just my nightdress and bare feet. What made me go I do not know, but I was compelled to run down the lane to the road.

'Oh my God no'. I shouted. It was Louise in the middle of the road and behind me was the sinister rumble of the carriage of Sir Hector.

'Louise' I shouted, but the words would not come out. I tried to run towards her, but my legs would not respond. I screamed in frustration at my body which seemed to be frozen solid. With a supreme effort I tried to move a single step, but couldn't and I collapsed into the mud. I lifted myself up, the rain and mud trickling down my face. Louise and the carriage were no more. I heard a strange hissing and rolling over in the mud I saw the buckled bonnet of my car emanating steam from a broken radiator. I collapsed once more into the mud and passed into a confusing world of swirling mist and unconsciousness.

I awoke in glaring light and pulsating noises with many voices of incessant chatter. My vision slowly cleared and a man's face began to materialise.

'Jed' I whispered.

'Gareth, if you please.

'Gareth, it's you'.

'You've been in a car crash'.

I felt physically drained and was unable to speak further, I fell exhausted into a deep sleep for several hours. The next time I awoke I was more coherent; the doctor informed me that I was suffering from concussion, but nothing too serious. Unfortunately however I had lost the baby I was carrying. Gareth's child, or was it Jed's. It was difficult to come to terms with the situation immediately and it was obviously going to take a long time to get myself together again.

Later that evening Gareth came to see me and it lifted my spirits immensely to see him. I told him about the baby and I just dissolved into tears. I felt reassured by his comforting and the doctor said that there was no reason why we could not have children in the future.

'One thing is puzzling me though Kate'. Said Gareth.

'Oh yes'.

'When the police found you lying in the mud...'

'Yes?'

'You were wearing an old fashioned nightdress'.

'Well I thought it would save time later'. That was the only feeble excuse I could think of on the spur of the moment. I certainly didn't feel up to explaining the whole story at this point in time.

A few days later I had Gareth drive me to the spot where the accident happened. He stayed in the car and I walked down the lane to the cottage. I was shocked to see it in ruins and felt a tear roll down my check. I went inside and stood in the spot that would have been the bedroom, looking out and imagining Jed swinging his axe and chopping wood. I could imagine myself there I could feel his warm lithe body again. I could feel him making love to me.

'Hello there'. Came a woman's voice from behind that abruptly bought me back to reality.

'Oh hello, I'm just looking'. I said, slightly startled.

'A nice place at one time'.

'Yes, I can imagine. Do you know what happened'?

'Oh rather, yes'. She said keenly. 'I work at the library in the archive department and I've been doing a local study'.

'What happened to the people who lived here'?

'Well a bit of a mystery actually. Hearsay has it that a gamekeeper lived here with his wife and that she mysteriously disappeared one night and was never seen again'.

'And the gamekeeper'?

'Well he was so distraught that he went to Africa and was never to return'.

I started to cry again.

'I say are you all right'?

'Yes please excuse me. It's a sad story'.

'Yes it is isn't it? Well if you are all right I'll press on'.

'Yes of course. Oh what about the old Manor over the high field'?

'Completely gone I'm afraid. It's a housing estate now. Progress I suppose'.

And with that she left. I wondered through to what was the yard and saw a piece of rusty metal. It was Jed's axe head. I wrapped it in a tissue and turned to go. A wind suddenly blew up and on the wind I heard a voice.

'I love you Kate'.

'I love you too'.

It was unmistakably Jed. I shivered as I remembered those magical mystical days and returned with my memento from that bygone age to the car and to Gareth and to the present.

INDULGENT WEEKEND

As we drove through the picturesque countryside everything felt right with the world. A luxurious weekend lay ahead of us, it was my birthday today and Simon had planned something special. Last night he took me to the theatre to see a fantastically funny play called *Lust In The Dust*, it was absolutely hilarious and I literally wet my panties with laughing so hard. It would cheer up the most miserable curmudgeon, I can highly recommend it.

Back to this weekend, Simon had booked for us, two days of pure hedonistic luxury at a very select country hotel. As we drove, his description of the forthcoming indulgence sounded absolutely wonderful, this place apparently had everything, sauna, Jacuzzi, gym, massage, volcanic mud treatment, the lot. We turned off the road and paused at the lodge gates. A uniformed security guard checked our booking and welcomed us through. The view took my breath away, it was a sweeping country estate, with fallow deer serenely grazing on a rolling meadow and further on, romantic ancient woods. A picture of perfect tranquillity in fact and I could feel myself being lulled into a state of perfect peace already.

We drove on, the birds were singing and in the distance you could make out the faint lowing of cattle. I could hear the sounds of a tennis match and as we rounded the bend to pass the courts it suddenly dawned on me that there was something Simon hadn't told me about this place. The foursome playing tennis were stark naked. I looked at Simon and he had a big knowing grin on his face. 'A nudist weekend.' I exclaimed.

'Yep'. He replied, with an air of nonchalance

Well it was something different I suppose. I watched the players as we slowly drove past and it occurred to me that whenever you see old pictures of naturist clubs, they were inevitably playing tennis and with lusting fascination, I could see why. A young firm bodied woman of about twenty five, gracefully served to a very buxom lady aged about forty five, which incidentally seemed also to be her bust size as well. She ran to receive the serve, her huge breasts bouncing and clapping together as she did so. She missed and her husband tried vainly to intercept the ball and as he did, his very generous, soft penis slapped against each thigh in turn. A game of tennis certainly highlights a person's soft wobbly body equipment.

So for the next forty eight hours, the security guard's uniform was going to be the last stitch of clothing we would see. Apart from meal times of course, when according to Simon, the management insisted that lower garments must be worn for hygiene reasons. Which was obvious really, plus there was always the danger of someone stabbing someone's sausage with their fork.

'What do you think Angie, do you like the look of the place?' Asked Simon as we drove up the long drive towards a truly magnificent mansion.

'I'm impressed, really impressed.' I replied, mouth agape.

Taking in the sheer splendour of the place, I assumed many years ago it was the residence of a Duke or some equally established dignitary. Now I don't know much about eighteenth century architecture, but you could tell that this place had history. We pulled into a parking bay at the front of the building and Simon took the cases from the car. Walking towards the entrance I marvelled at its sheer majesty, this was going to be some weekend.

I felt like royalty as we walked up the wide stone steps, past the marble pillars of the portico and in through the large grand doors into the entrance hall. The ceiling, way above us, was painted with ancient gods draped in silk robes. They appeared to be flying through a sky of cloud and battle scenes, and were flanked by trumpet blowing cherubs. There was an imposing staircase that led to a galleried landing before us which was adorned with very old paintings, the largest portrait of which bore a striking resemblance to the central god on the ceiling. A piece of vanity of the highest order I suppose, probably depicting the former owner of this palace and was aimed to impress his guests.

There was no one on the reception desk, so Simon rang the bell. A few seconds later a young athletic woman skipped down the central staircase. Naked of course and her petite firm breasts gently bobbed as she descended the stairs. She had long blond straight hair with a fringe cut just above her eyebrows. Pale blue eyes and an angelic face with a peach complexion. Her wide hips and athletic thighs, drew your eyes to her shaved pussy, the lips of which seemed very full and inviting, especially to Simon who was staring at it, no doubt imagining those firm cunt lips sucking his ever eager cock. The girl noticed and looked down at herself, brushing imaginary fluff from her tummy, which gave an even greater inclination to look at her pubescent magnificence.

'Hi I'm Pru. Mr and Mrs Dale, is it?' She asked.

I nudged Simon in the ribs with my elbow to bring him back to earth.

'Oh, yes, it is.' He said with a grunt as he rubbed his chest.

'You'll have to forgive him. I've told him before not to stare.' I said.

'That's alright; bodies are there to be looked at.' She replied, with a casual matter of fact air. 'Here are your keys, room thirty two, on the first floor. Up the stairs and to your left. It's a lovely room with a good view of the grounds. I'm sure you'll find it most comfortable.'

'I'm sure we will.' Said Simon, still staring at her pussy.

'And when you have settled in I will give you a tour of the complex and outline our services and facilities.' She continued.

I took his arm and pulled him away, his eyes still bulging. We went to our room and quickly unpacked. I could tell Simon was anxious to see the place, or rather the people in it and I must admit I did fancy some of the treatments on offer; the only problem was which to choose first.

I noticed the information pack had a leaflet headed "All Tastes Catered For" I was about to read it thinking, rather naively as it turned out, that it was the menu. I was later to find out what "All Tastes Catered For", really meant.

We both stripped off and threw our clothes onto the bed. The room had French windows that led onto a balcony and I couldn't resist it. I walked through onto the balcony and sighed as I felt the warm sun caress my breasts. Simon followed me out and from behind, put his arms around me and took my breasts in his hands. I was proud of my figure, everything was in proportion and my breasts were firm, as Simon was discovering, but not too large. As he fondled me, my nipples were becoming erect with the erotic sensation. 'Steady on.' I said brushing his hands away. 'We've just got here. You can't go walking about with a hard on. What would the other guests think?'

'Oh yes, I never thought about that. What am I going to do if I'm talking to some fantastically sexy woman and I start getting erect?' He said worriedly.

'You'll have to keep a shoulder bag with you and if it happens, you'll have to hold it in front of your cock.' I replied.

Going down the grand staircase to the reception I felt very regal indeed. There were a few people of various ages and shapes milling about and as I walked down the stairs I purposely made my breasts bounce. It turned a few heads and I felt myself being watched as I exaggerated my movement, making them swing and wobble for their pleasure. It was an exhilarating and liberating experience. The reception was empty again and Simon rang the bell to summon Pru's pussy. I heard the sound of chatter and giggling and turned to see two couples coming down the stairs. They seemed to be sauntering down slowly for effect and attention, as I had just done, and looking at them it was obvious why. They put my little saunter to shadow and the attraction was the two men. Their penises were huge; they knew it and they flaunted it. One of them in particular, a six foot two blond Scandinavian looking Adonis, had a cock that was as big as a babies leg, with balls like the ones we had seen on the tennis court earlier. As they messed around on the stairs it shook and whipped around his thighs and I couldn't take my eyes off it. His bulbous end just cheekily peeking out half an inch from his foreskin and it looked very enticing. The rest of his bell end was covered by his foreskin, but you could clearly see the out line of that tantalising rim. That rim of the glans that stimulates your G-spot so erotically, I thought to myself. I pictured myself gently pulling back his foreskin to reveal that huge purple pulsating globe of pleasure. What must it be like when it's fully erect and in full majesty, I thought with a sigh? The other man was darker and more thickly set. His shaft was not quite as big but very generous for all that, plus he was circumcised, showing off his purple head, which was a big mouthful by anyone's standard. And the women? Well their physical attributes were pleasant, but not outstanding. The only thing they seemed to have that was big, was the smiles on their faces and given their partners huge cocks, you could understand why. I sighed once more as the penises disappeared through the door marked "Pleasures". In a dream I turned to the reception desk to see that Simon was already talking to Pru's shaven haven. Between themselves they had arranged the promised tour of the premises.

Pru took us through the door marked "Pleasures" and down a long corridor of doors, all marked with the delights Simon had mentioned on the way here.

'Would you like a video record of your visit?' Asked Pru. 'Most of our guests take up the option, it's very popular.' She continued.

'What is it?' Asked Simon.

'It simply means that there are cameras discretely positioned in certain of the pleasure rooms and your treatment or "special tastes" are filmed and edited by our expert video technicians and for a small charge you have a DVD record of your visit to enjoy at your leisure.'

I wasn't so sure, as I had visions of one of the neighbours telling me that they'd seen a porno film with someone in it who looked remarkably like me.

'Sounds great.' Beamed Simon enthusiastically. 'We'll go for that.'

'Er, well, I don't know.' I stammered.

'Nothing to worry about,' reassured Pru, 'its very discreet, come, I'll show you.'

She led us through a door marked "private". In there were a bank of televisions and she switched them on.

'This is our video and editing suite, all state of the art equipment and today one of our "special tastes" room is being used by Mr. and Mrs. Ford. Now normally this would be for their private use, but the Fords are exhibitionists and it gives them greater enjoyment in their activities if they know they are being watched. In fact the film we are now making for them is to be publicly screened on Thursday evening in the ballroom.'

The monitors showed the Fords in what seemed to be a classroom of the nineteen sixties. Mrs. Ford, who seemed a very small woman of about thirty with large lensed glasses, was dressed in a black teacher's gown and had a matching mortar board on her head. She had one of those old fashioned school canes with a rounded handle like a small flexible walking stick. She was bending it menacingly and pointing to simple, very simple mathematical calculations written in white chalk on a large blackboard that stood on an easel next to her desk, the whole assembly of which was on a slightly elevated stage. The camera viewpoints gave us an all round impression of the room. Mr Ford, who by contrast to his wife seemed a very large man and was sitting at a small desk, pen in hand and exercise book open. He seemed rather scantily clad, as were we all, wearing a green and yellow peaked cap, a starched collar, without shirt attached and a small green and yellow tie that matched the cap. To complete the ensemble he wore thick, grey knee high socks and large clumpy black shoes. She tapped the blackboard with her cane then stepped off her stage and came to look what her husband had written.

She stood over him, then slammed her cane down hard onto his desk. He jumped in terror.

'Wrong, boy'. She screamed like a demented harpy. 'Two and two make four, not five.'

'Sorry Miss.' He snivelled.

'Sorry! Not good enough. Come to the front to be punished.'

Mr Ford got up and cowered towards the blackboard. He was a huge man of about six foot six and two hundred and eighty pounds. He also had a huge dangly penis that wobbled from side to side as he shuffled towards the blackboard. She pointed aggressively to the two plus two written on the board.

'What's the answer boy?'

'Five Miss.' He said timidly.

'Wrong.' She bellowed. 'Hands on the top of the board you evil little maggot.'

He reached up and gripped each corner of the board, shivering in terror. The teacher removed her glasses, took off her mortar board and placed them on her desk, her cane placed alongside, She then shrugged of her gown, letting it slide from her shoulders and fall to the floor. She was naked. Although a small woman she was very shapely, with broad round hips and for her size, very large breasts. She must have been at least a forty four inch F cup, which meant her figure was eye-catching to say the least. Because of how proudly her breasts stuck out, I suspected that she must have had some surgical augmentation. She let loose her hair, which was in a roll at the back of her head and she shook it free which also made her breasts wobble and shake slightly, much to Simons pleasure. With her beautiful figure and long dark hair she certainly was a very attractive woman. She then picked up her cane and flexed it.

'You've been a bad boy Roger, haven't you?' She said walking up and down behind him, still flexing her cane.

'Yes Miss.' Whimpered Roger.

With that she turned rapidly on her heels and gave Roger an almighty lash across his buttocks, her breasts tightening and lurching with the effort of the stroke. The sound of the cane sounded like a bullwhip and Roger screamed out and his body tautened with the impact.

'Can't hear you Roger.'

'Yes Miss.' He said louder, almost crying with pain.

'Don't, dare, raise your voice to me boy.' She barked back, her tits shaking as she raised the cane for another stroke, which came down again on Rogers's backside.

His buttocks tightened with the lash and he stifled a whimper as his knuckles showed white as he gripped the corners of the blackboard.

'We don't like dunces at this school do we Roger?'

'No Miss.'

And with that she landed another blow on his buttocks which were now beginning to glow with the clearly visible lash marks. His body once again winced with pain.

'Now then Roger, I shall ask again, what is two plus two?'

'Five Miss?'

'Wrong.'

And again her tits heaved as she swung another lash to poor Roger's buttocks.

'Three Miss?'

'Wrong again.'

And down came the lash. Roger screamed out in agony, his backside now a mass of red and white lines. How much can he stand I thought.

'Two plus two Roger, what is it?'

'Is it four Miss?' He whimpered.

'Don't you know?' She said with sarcastic menace and whipped him again.

Roger screamed out in agony once more.

'It's four Miss. Definitely four.' He blurted out through gritted teeth and hanging exhausted against the blackboard.

'Very good. You have been a good boy and good boys get rewards. Turn round Roger.'

Roger, a broken man, turned to face her. What was interesting about his experience was that when he turned around he had a huge erection which must have been eight inches long, so his ordeal can't have been that unpleasant.

'Do you want your reward for being a good little boy Roger?'

'Oh yes please Miss.' He said with joy.

With that she kneeled down in front of him and took hold of his enormous shaft and kissed his huge purple end. Roger groaned with pleasure.

'Suck me Miss, suck me.' He said almost childishly.

The teacher began to take his shaft into her mouth. It was wide open and only just fitted in. Her mouth slid slowly down his shaft and although only a small women she was able to take in most of his length. She then drew back, his cock glistening with her saliva. She then started her down stroke and his cock slowly entered her mouth again.

'More Miss, more.' Begged Roger as he grasped the back of her head urging more of his manhood into her throat. Back and forth she went and Roger was getting very sexually excited. She sucked his huge glans and at the same time rubbed up and down his cock with her hand. Roger was about to climax.

'Oh Miss I'm coming.' He screamed.

He took her head and she gripped his hips. Roger forced his cock deep into her mouth, pulled back and forced her mouth onto him again. He was now in control and gripping her head and her tits shaking uncontrollably she was at his mercy. On and on he went forcing his cock into her until he let out an almighty scream and all his pent up semen shot into the teacher's mouth. She gasped as he continued to mouth fuck her. His shaft was coated in his sticky semen and as he continued to pump her, it oozed out from the corner of her mouth. Breathing heavily and lust sated, he pushed the teacher to the floor and she lay there dazed with a trickle of semen running from the corner of her mouth.

'Well, there you are,' said Pru, switching off the monitors, 'end of part one.'

'You mean there's more.' Said I.

'Oh yes. They will be at it for some time. Mrs Ford hasn't had her orgasm yet. We'll send you a copy of the DVD if you like.'

'Yes please do.' I replied.

Simon coughed nervously.

'Are you alright?'

'Fine.'

Pru and I looked simultaneously at Simon's erection.

'I could recommend a massage. It's very good for relieving stiffness.' Said Pru with a glint in her eye.

'Do you have a masseur free?' Asked Roger.

'Yes. Me actually.' Said Pru.

Roger looked at me pleadingly.

'Go to it.' I said.

I knew he was aching to get inside Pru's tight little cunt, so I left them to it and I went to check out the swimming pool and any talent that might be around.

It was only a small swimming pool and I had it all to myself and swam leisurely up and down. Then I heard the door open and in walked the blond Adonis I had seen on the stairs earlier. He was alone and he walked in with his massive trunk of a penis swaying between his legs. I rolled over on my back and did a sort of breaststroke in reverse. I was swimming away from him so he had a clear view of my legs opening. A bit blatant I know but still.

'Hello.' He said.

'Hello.' I replied, unable to take my eyes of his enormous shaft and swimming towards him for a closer look.

'I'm Clive.' He said.

I reached the pool side and stood up in the four foot deep water. I pushed my hair back with both hands and shook my head to make my breasts shake for him.

'I'm Angie.' I replied.

He bent forward with his left hand on his thigh and offered his right hand to me. It was indecently close to his penis and I took it eagerly.

'Pleased to meet you Angie.'

'And you too.' I replied

As I shook his hand I let my wrist brush against his manhood.

'Oh I'm terribly sorry.' I said, feigning shock.

'It's quite alright. It's always getting in the way.'

'You should put it somewhere then.' I said, surprised at my own forwardness.

'Yes maybe I should.' He replied.

A feeling came over me and I thought if you don't ask you don't get, so I took the pull by the horns. I mean at this very moment Simon's shaft is probably exploring the delights of Pru's shaven cunt, so I took a deep breath and went for it. 'Can I ask you something?' I said looking at this magnificent penis.

'Certainly, anything.'

'Would you pull your foreskin back for me?'

To my surprise he did exactly that and without even flinching, almost as if he was asked to do it every day. He took his cock between thumb and forefinger and slowly pulled back his foreskin to reveal the biggest bell end I have ever seen. The rim of it where it met his shaft stood proud and I thought of it sliding inside me. I was stunned to silence and because of the attention it was getting, his shaft was becoming erect.

'Do you like what you see?' He asked.

'Oh you bet.' I replied unable to take my eyes off it.

He rubbed his hand up and down its length and with every stroke it seemed to get an inch longer. I watched in wonderment as this thing hardened and lengthened before me. It was an absolute wondrous sight. He continued to rub his shaft and soon it was like a ram rod, stiff as a flagpole and rock hard and throbbing. It was aching for a home and I was aching to give it one, it was all of ten inches long, ten inches of pulsating cock.

I pushed myself away from the side and floated on my back with my legs open. Clive stood on the side looking at me.

'Well?' I said.

And I didn't need to say anything more. Clive jumped into the pool and took me into his arms and kissed me passionately. I could feel my cunt was wet with passion and aching for it. I didn't need any foreplay; I had had a whole day of foreplay. I just wanted Clive's cock inside me.

'Fuck me Clive.' I begged.

Supported by the water I put my legs around his waist. With one hand around his neck I took his cock with the other one and guided it into my hungry cunt. It was absolutely massive and I wondered if I could take a monster of this size. I felt my flesh being stretched open as Clive gently slid inside me. I felt my whole cunt being forced apart as inch by inch this huge cock entered my body. It sort of hurt, but it was a hurt every woman wants, the hugest cock in the world inside her cunt. Onwards he thrust until it reached inside me and would go no further.

'Fuck me Clive. Fuck me like there's no tomorrow.' I begged.

He took hold of my hips and fucked me so hard it hurt, an exquisite pain of ultimate pleasure. In and out he went and my cunt sucked hard onto his shaft as he pulled out and then he gripped my hips as he pulled me down hard onto his cock, the shaft slamming into me, his huge dagger of pleasure stabbing me deeply inside. Pain and pleasure together it was ecstasy. On every stroke his bell rim slid past my clitoris exciting me to higher levels of pleasure on every thrust, and then his huge rim rasped my G-spot giving me double pleasure. On and on he thrust making us boil with pleasure and on and on his shaft rubbed my clitoris to the point of no return. One more thrust was all it needed to send me to heavenly orgasm and I screamed as he delivered that momentous stroke, a thrust that went deep inside me, deep inside my cunt, deep inside my very soul. I just exploded with pleasure and Clive continued to slam his mighty shaft inside me. My cunt gripped his cock, sucking it to submission as convulsions of ultimate pleasure ripped through my body. I could feel his cock pulsate and ripple inside me and I knew he was coming. He yelled out as his semen shot inside me. My cunt sucked this throbbing monster, sucking the love juice out of it, sucking this beast inside me. My cunt devoured him and sucked him dry. Clive slid from me and drifted in the water. My cunt was victorious.

WORKING FOR THE FIRM

⟨∞⟩

This was the day; I awoke with a feeling of nervousness and excitement. I was starting a new job with a company that is known locally as *"The Firm"*. The company had a reputation for secrecy; its day to day workings were shrouded in a veil of mystery. They were one of the biggest employers in the area, but what they produced no one seemed to know. They had large administration offices and an even larger warehouse, the contents of which were a mystery and to be honest, were of no interest to me anyway as I would be working in the offices. I knew a number of people who worked there, but none would talk about their work or the company to outsiders. The discipline of company confidentiality was of paramount importance and anyone found guilty of breaching that confidentiality was dealt with severely. The company never advertised a vacancy, or needed to for that matter, because no one had ever been known to leave of their own free will. No one to my knowledge, or anyone else's knowledge had ever been dismissed either, because the employment was so lucrative no employee dared to jeopardise their job. In fact the only time a position became available was due either to retirement or death. And even then replacements were only made through the nomination and recommendation from existing staff. So I was lucky and had been nominated by Jane, a long time friend with whom I went to school.

The firm did have a name, but rarely ever used and it was always referred to as "the firm". Apart from the air of mystery and strict secrecy about the place, the only other thing that was known to outsiders was that they paid very good salaries. In fact like for like, they paid twice as much as its nearest rival, who also had a reputation for paying very good money. So everyone wanted to work for *the firm* and this was to be my first day. I had not even set foot in the building yet, as the job selection and interviews had taken place at the offices of a company that dealt in the recruitment and placing of specialist staff.

Better get up and get moving, I thought, don't want to be late on my first day. Brian, my partner was already up and had left for work and I kissed his pillow and smiled to myself as I thought about the electric sex of last night and as I threw back the duvet to reveal my naked body I could smell that beautiful musty aroma of Brian's passion within me. I showered and dressed. It was forecast to be a warm day so I dressed accordingly in a light cotton yellow floral print dress and white cardigan. I had an all over delicate honey tan so didn't need to wear tights, which made for greater comfort. I looked at myself in the mirror, not bad I thought, smart but casual, this outfit showed my figure off well. I considered myself lucky, I had always had a trim well proportioned figure and I didn't have to fight with it to keep it under control like a lot of girls did. My breasts weren't as big as I would have liked, but Brian always said, that anything more than a handful was a waste, so if it pleased him, that was OK by me. A last flick with the brush through my shoulder length blond hair, not forgetting my fringe and with a blue hair band, which was more for show than purpose, I was ready. So with butterflies in my tummy I set off for work. I went by train and this part of the line was always quiet so I had a compartment to myself and was able to contemplate the day ahead.

I arrived at *the firm* and it looked a very imposing building. Other staff members were arriving and they looked cheerful enough, some almost seemingly to be skipping to work. That's reassuring I thought to myself as a lot of places that I have worked, people were going in as if they were about to face the gallows. Taking a deep breath I entered and reported to the reception. 'Cathy Boyd,' I said to the smiling receptionist, 'I'm starting work today.'

'Ah yes,' she said, looking at a list and ticking off my name, 'please take a seat, your supervisors will be down shortly.'

She indicated a sofa and I joined a young man who was sitting nervously waiting for his supervisor, I assumed. We smiled at each other. Quite a nice looking chap I thought, I could really fancy him. I wondered if he would be in my department, I'd like to get to know him better. 'Pull yourself together Cathy,' I told myself, here I was on the verge of a new career and I was eying up the talent.

'First day?' He ventured.

'Yes.' I replied.

'John Page.' He said offering his hand. 'I'm going to be in accounts.'

'Cathy Boyd.' I replied, taking his hand. Accounts eh, well we wouldn't be working together after all, I thought to myself. Never mind perhaps I could catch him later.

Before we could start a conversation a tall military looking gentleman with a neatly trimmed moustache entered and approached us.

'Mr Page.' He enquired with an authoritative but pleasant voice.

'Yes.' He replied nervously and automatically standing to attention.

'Come this way please.'

The military man about turned sharply and John shuffled after him and quietly wished me 'good luck,' as he departed.

A lift door hissed open and out stepped two women, they looked at me and in perfect step they approached. Their appearance was somewhat disconcerting. They looked very serious, they both had black straight hair that was just less than shoulder length and parted in the middle and both had very dark eyes, which were made more pronounced by their makeup. They were of average height, but broad and thick set, not fat by any means, but well rounded with wide hips and large busts. Both were wearing identical two piece suits that were made out of a thick olive colored material and their outfits were finished off with heavy brogue shoes. They didn't have any blouses on under their jackets and both displayed very ample cleavages, and despite their stern appearances, that put me in mind of two KGB officers, they were both very attractive looking women, in fact they were of so similar appearance, they could have been twins.

'Miss Boyd.' Said one and I found myself standing to attention just as John had done.

'Yes.' I replied with a slight trembling in my voice, which I quickly cleared.

'I'm Clara Henderson and this is my sister June, welcome to the firm.' She said and confirmed my guess about them being siblings. We shook hands.

'As this is your first day, it will be spent mainly in the induction process, demonstrating the company work process, history, fire and safety regulations etc.' Continued Clara.

'But first and foremost you will be inducted into the company policy of brotherhood and rewards and discipline.' Added June with something of a sinister little smile on her face.

'Follow us please.' Barked Clara.

They both turned as one and walked off in step. I followed, trying to keep in step. We entered the lift and as we did so someone who I assumed was the internal mail delivery boy was also about to enter. Clara gave him a cool stare and he backed away. The lift ascended with the three of us. The KGB sisters, as I had named them, were certainly an authority within this new world I had entered and as the lift went higher and higher my blood chilled at the thought of the "policy of brotherhood, rewards and discipline". Whatever did that mean? The lift stopped abruptly at the eighth floor and I couldn't help but notice Clara and June's huge breasts bounce magnificently. The door slid open.

'Step out please.' Ordered June.

I did so and with one either side of me we marched down a seemingly endless corridor.

'Most people, Miss Boyd, when they join the company, invariably stay here for the rest of their lives and we hope you to will be one of our faithful associates.' Said Clara.

'Yes I hope so too.' I replied.

'Of course as well as the induction course, we will require you to take some simple psychological tests to confirm your aptitude for your career ahead.' Followed on June.

'Tests?' I questioned nervously.

'Nothing to worry about, nobody has failed yet. In fact after the initial, shall we say surprise of its rather unorthodox nature, most candidates claim it was a life enhancing exercise. Of course no test is ever the same, it is always tailored to the candidate's psychological profile.' Continued Clara.

'Lovely headband.' Remarked June with a reassuring smile.

'Oh thank you.' I replied, a little taken aback by this affectionate gesture.

We stopped suddenly and June opened a door, again as she did so I couldn't help noticing the mobility of her bosom and assumed that neither of them were wearing bras.

I entered the dimly lit room with a little trepidation. It seemed to be empty except for a table in the middle. June turned up the lights slightly and closed the door, turning the key, which she then put into her pocket.

'We don't want to be disturbed do we?' She said in a sinister voice that made me very nervous.

'Stand at the foot of the altar.' Said Clara, pointing to the table.

The word altar made my blood run cold and although fear was creeping over me I felt compelled to obey. I stood at the end of this table. It had tubular metal legs and the top was about seven feet long and about four feet wide. Its surface was covered with what appeared to be red padded leather, stitched and studded in diamond shapes. There appeared to be drawers underneath and things dangling that because of the gloom I could not make out. The top of the table came up to the top of my thighs. I was transfixed with a sort of cold fear. Clara and June stood either side of me. I wanted to speak but could not. Each took hold of my arms and pulled me forward roughly and my chest and face slammed into the soft leather surface of the altar. My wrists were wrenched forward and I felt something grip them. I looked up through my tousled hair and I could see the KGB sisters fastening straps that were attached to chains around my wrist. I was still winded from hitting the top of the altar and was unable to get my breath, or to speak. By now I was becoming really frightened. I felt my legs being forced apart and my ankles being bound with leather manacles. I was trapped and completely unable to move, at the mercy of these beasts.

'Your first test my dear.' Said Clara.

She then nodded to June. She was behind me and she roughly lifted up my dress and pulled it halfway up my back, then wrenched down my knickers. Because my legs were open and shackled they only went halfway down my thighs. Oh God, what are they going to do to me?

'She's ready.' Said June.

'I should mention that the room is completely sound proof so please feel free to make any noises you feel necessary, your screams won't be disturbing anyone.' Said Clara and as she did so she slid open a drawer just under my face and my blood ran cold when I saw what was inside. There were huge serrated knives, huge things that were like pliers and huge metal bars covered in soot and that had obviously been in a fire and heated to great temperatures. I felt sick with fear. Clara fumbled through these instruments of torture and pulled out a multi lashed whip. Then slid the drawer shut. In silence she walked out of my eye line. I began to cry, what had I let myself in for, will I ever see Brian again. In the silence I waited for the inevitable, I could hear Clara separating the strands of the whip. I heard her take in a deep breath to gain maximum force for her lash. I heard the whistle of air as the lash of the whip hissed through the air and slapped onto my naked flesh. It hurt, it really hurt and I bit my bottom lip to stifle a cry. Clara snorted as she drew back the lash. I winced again as the next blow made contact with my bare bottom. The third blow struck me and I felt one of the lashes hit my pussy making my lips tingle. And another, again caressing the lips of my pussy. I t was now glowing and tingling. Then the tenth lash came down as mercilessly as the first and my buttocks and pussy felt as though they should be on fire.

'That's enough.' Ordered June.

I lay there breathing heavily, my backside and my pussy was glowing and tingling. Then I realised that the pain was in my mind, the whip was not leather but a sort of light polyester. I heard the sisters sniggering.

'They all fall for it.' Said Clara with tongue in cheek. 'The mind is a powerful thing, it believes what it thinks it sees'.

June opened the drawer again and took out a pewter jewel encrusted jar. She unscrewed the lid to reveal cold cream; she took a generous scoop out and started to rub it onto my glowing buttocks. It felt cool and refreshing as she massaged it into me. I lay there in submission of pleasure, still manacled to the altar while June continued with her massage.

Clara watched silently and as I looked up and smiled she began to slowly unbutton her jacket and as I surmised earlier she wasn't wearing a bra. She slid the jacket from her shoulders and let it fall to the floor. I must admit her breasts were magnificently huge and it was very erotic to watch her caressing and fondling them. She let her hands follow their contours with unbelievable eroticism. This performance was for me and as she moaned gently and looked skyward in sexual pleasure June continued to work on me. I felt her fingers exploring further and felt them go between my legs. I could feel my pussy tingling, partly because of the whipping and partly because they yearned for stimulation. I wanted June's fingers to touch me and I was enthralled by Clara's sexual ritual. She now went further and unzipped her skirt and let it drop. She was wearing the briefest of blue panties which she slowly slid down her thighs, bending towards me and letting he huge tits dangle and shake. She looked at me with such yearning I could tell she wanted me as much as I wanted her. She kicked away her knickers and her shoes and stood naked. She shook her tits for me again then let her hands follow the shape of her body. Her body was magnificent, a narrow waist and very wide hips which she caressed then let her left hand slide across her belly. Her eyes looked up at mine as she let her hand drift down to her pussy. I saw her gasp as her fingers slide between her legs. And I gasped, as simultaneously June's fingers slid across my vulva and touched my clitoris.

Then, in what seemed like a mere second I was unshackled, standing upright, my dress unzipped and off, my bra unclipped and off and my knickers finishing their journey down my thighs. I was naked, as was June and she looked identical to her sister. Somehow the altar had been lowered and I was lying on my back. June was kneeling, her face between my thighs and kissing my clitoris. Clara was straddling my shoulders and looking up I could see her beautiful face smiling down at me between her breasts. She held her cunt open as she lowered herself onto my waiting tongue. I did not disappoint her and I clutched her thighs as my tongue went to work on her eager clitoris, licking her into a frenzy of pleasure.

June was doing the same to me. She lifted my legs over her shoulder and with my legs folded around her neck I pulled her into my aching little cunt, a cunt that wanted licking to orgasm. As June licked me, I licked Clara and as I licked her she slid her hips back and forth gently as she fucked me. I could see her tits swaying above me and it gave me even greater pleasure. I could feel June licking me and I could feel the pleasure rising to the point of no return. I started to moan and June sensed I was close and gripped my thighs harder and licked my clit faster and faster. It was overwhelming me, I was coming. In turn I gripped and licked Clara with greater passion and I could tell by how she was breathing and how her tits were shaking that she too was coming. It was here, it was happening, I was coming. June licked harder and faster and clutched my thighs holding me down on the altar. Both Clara and I exploded into an uproarious orgasm simultaneously. My fingers dug into the flesh of her thighs as I forced her cunt into my mouth and sucked out her love juice.

Clara and June got up and filled in some details on a clip board.

'Well Cathy,' said June, 'I'm pleased to tell you that you have passed the first test with flying colors. Welcome to *The Firm*.

What a first day it had been. I sat in the train compartment that evening with a big smile on my face, the first day successfully over. Before the train pulled away I was joined by a handsome young man with an equally big smile on his face. It was John Page. He had obviously had a similar day to me. I couldn't wait to see what tomorrow would bring.

DELIVERED IN ERROR

The sun was shining, through the cherry blossom and as the petals began to fall in the light breeze, they cascaded down like a myriad tiny butterflies. It was one of those days that made you feel glad to be alive. I had just had a bath and I stood in the living room in my robe admiring the view and taking stock of my life. In some ways I was very lucky, I had a part time job, which I loved and being only three days a week gave me plenty of time for gardening and my music. Financially, I was comfortably off and the house was paid for. On the negative side I was lonely, at least for some of the time. I was a widow of eight years and was on the wrong side of fifty, but pleasant looking, or so I've been told, but my body was beginning to spread and my bust which was also approaching fifty in both years and inches, sagged somewhat. Oh well, that's my lot I suppose, things could be worse. I lived on a small but very pleasant housing estate, which unlike most estates these days the houses were spread comfortably so you had a sense of space. My house was at the top of a cul-de-sac so there was no traffic noise.

Looking down the avenue I saw Michael walking up the hill. Michael was a very pleasant young man from the other side of the estate. He had delivered our newspapers faithfully, in all weathers for many years until moving onto college and then presumably university. He was a good looking boy with a very girlish face, now I don't mean that in a derogatory way, it's just that he looked pretty rather than rugged and handsome. But there again he must only be about nineteen so let us all enjoy his boyish charm. He had been dating a lovely girl called Andrea and they made a lovely couple, childhood sweethearts I believe. I could see that he had an envelope in his hands and I knew it had been delivered in error. This was a mistake partly due to the planners who had named the streets. I lived at Belmont Avenue number twenty and Michael lived in Belmont Close number twenty. So this sort of occurrence was not uncommon.

Michael approached the gate and I made sure my robe was properly fastened and went to the front door to meet him. He smiled his lovely warm smile as he entered and as he walked up the drive I couldn't help thinking what a lovely young man he was. His hair was short and well groomed, baby blue eyes and he always had rosy cheeks, almost angelic He had a sort of childlike innocence about him, almost an aura of vulnerability. That was probably what made him so attractive, I wanted to mother and protect him from this wicked world. Then I thought, what am I thinking of, I should be ashamed of myself, this young boy of nineteen is almost young enough to be my grandchild.

As Michael walked up the drive he tripped and fell headlong onto the path. I rushed out to assist and help him to his feet.

'I'm terribly sorry Mrs. Booth; you must think I'm a clumsy fool.' He said apologetically.

'Oh Michael are you alright?' I said as I steadied him.

'Perfectly thank you. I've just bought this letter for you. It came to our house by mistake.'

'That's very good of you Michael, thank you.'

'No trouble at all.'

As he handed me the envelope I could see that he had badly grazed the inside of his right forearm, near to his elbow. It must have caused him great discomfort but he showed no signs of complaining.

'You've hurt your arm Michael.' I said.

'It's nothing.' He said dismissively.

'Come inside and let me put something on it.'

'It's alright honestly.'

' Now come on, I insist.'

And I took him by his good elbow and led him in and through to the kitchen. I sat him down and filled a small bowl with warm water and found cotton wool and bottle of germicide from the cupboard to treat his wound. I pulled up a chair opposite Michael and soaked a swab of cotton wool in the water to clean any dirt from around his graze.

'This is very good of you Mrs. Booth.'

I thought it was charmingly respectful that he called me Mrs. Booth, Most youngsters these days seemed to have dispelled with any respect and formality towards the older generation. It made me think of many years ago when I was a young girl; it was the norm then to call adults Mr. and Mrs.

'That's perfectly alright Michael,' I said replying to his statement, 'but please call me Sarah.'

'Oh, right. Thank you, Sarah.' He said as if trying the name for size.

I bathed his wound a few times with the clean water and tried to get a conversation going. 'How are you and Andrea getting on?' I asked. He didn't answer immediately but just coughed. I looked up at him and he was blushing beautifully. I thought what a wonderfully sensitive boy; my probing question has embarrassed him.

'Er, I'm afraid we parted some months ago.' He stammered and then coughed again.

'Oh, I'm sorry to hear that. You've been together for some years haven't you?'

'Five.' He said with a hint of regret in his voice.

I had cleaned his graze and looking into his face he was still blushing.

'I'm sorry if my questions have made you feel uncomfortable.' I said apologetically.

'Sarah.' He said seriously.

'Yes?'

He then nodded as if to draw my attention to something. I looked down and to my horror my robe had come open and I was sitting opposite Michael exposing everything I had and with my legs wide open as well. I hastened to make myself decent and now I could feel my face going bright red as well.

'Oh Michael, I'm so sorry, what must you think?' I said feeling absolutely terrible.

'Well Sarah, I think you have an absolutely beautiful body and it was worth the agony of falling over to see it.' He replied.

'Er, thank you Michael.' I was still feeling embarrassed but I was immensely flattered by his compliments. 'I'll just dab on a little germicide lotion and I think you'll be OK.' I poured a little of the lotion on a cotton wool swab and took his arm at the back of his elbow. 'Now this may sting a little.'

Michael winced and as his arm shook, his hand touched my breast. Neither of us moved. His hand still on my breast I looked into his eyes and he into mine. We did not need to speak, our eyes said it all. Michael stood up and leaned forward and kissed me, his hand now gently caressing my breast. I felt feelings stirring within me, feelings I had not felt for many years. What shall I do? I knew the carnal thoughts that were running through my mind were wrong, but the urge was strong, so very strong. I took a long slow breathe of air and as he kissed me, I had decided, I wanted this young man to make love to me. I gently took his hand from my breast and led him upstairs to my bed. I let his hand go and walked in and stood by the bed. I turned and Michael was framed in the doorway. This angelic little boy was now a man before me. I undid the belt of my robe and with a shrug of my shoulders it fell to the floor. Michael stared in awe. I knew I was far from beautiful. My huge breasts sagged almost to my waist but I could see they had a fascination for Michael. I put my hands high on my chest and let them slide slowly down my breasts, gently caressing them, my fingers slowly flowing over my nipples which were now very hard and erect. His eyes were like saucers and he gasped. I performed for his delight for a little longer, then I held my arms open and I slowly and erotically said in a deep alluring voice. 'Fuck me Michael. Fuck me hard.'

He slowly and gracefully lifted his t-shirt above his head to reveal a very muscular and lithe torso. Then his jeans socks and trainers were removed with equal grace. Slowly he inserted his fingers into the waist band of his shorts and the final barrier was lowered. He stepped out of them and the sight was unbelievable. He was built like an Olympic athlete, this angelic little boy stood like a Greek god before me. He let his hands cascade down the rippling muscles of his body and he took his erect, pulsating manhood in his hands and stroked it along its entire eight inch length. It was beautiful, hard and erect and I needed it inside me.

Gracefully as a gazelle Michael glided towards me, taking me into his strong arms he kissed me like I had never been kissed before. He squeezed me so hard I could hardly breathe. I could feel his rock hard ramrod pressing into my tummy as his hand found my breast and fondled it lovingly, his fingers teasing my nipples to even greater erection. His strong hands then clutched my buttocks, pulling them apart which made my quim tingle and open. Like the giant he was, Michael put one hand behind my back and the other behind my thighs and swept me up as if I was weightless and gently laid me on the bed. I looked up at him wantonly as he looked down at me with sexual hunger in his eyes, a fierce hunger I knew he would satisfy. He kneeled beside me on the bed and gently kissed me, then he kissed and sucked my breasts in turn, holding one in both his hands and trying to get as much as possible inside his mouth. I loved it, every suck, every bite, and every caress.

He kissed lower and lower, down my belly, further and further. Still kneeling beside me his exploring kisses found my pussy. His lips found my lips. I could feel them opening for him and I shuddered with delight as he kissed them. I reached between Michaels legs and found his mighty shaft. He groaned with pleasure as I stroked and explored it length, then playing gently with his testicles, letting them flow between my fingers and gently shuffling them before returning to the worship of his mighty cock. Michael's tongue gently slid between my lips parting them slightly, it was an unbelievable feeling, and a sexual act that I had not experienced before and it excited me greatly. Michaels head between my legs and his tongue explored further, travelling down between my lips until it reached my tunnel of love, and then he pushed his tongue inside my womanhood. It was an unbelievable experience. His tongue then passed between my lips again until it reached my clitoris. I cried out with pleasure as his tongue passed over. Michael knew he had found the spot and he concentrated on it, licking it slowly and purposely, up and down and round and round. It was sending me to new heights of sexual rapture and as he did so, I caressed Michaels throbbing cock. The rhythm of Michael licking my clitoris was beginning to build into wild passion within me. I could feel it taking a grip of me, I was beginning to breathe heavily and Michael sensed this. His tongue exquisitely torturing me, his head buried within my thighs and his arms around them pulling my vagina open wide for his pleasure. I could feel my orgasm building to an almighty crescendo. 'Faster Michael lick me faster.' I pleaded. He ignored me, he cruelly ignored me. My orgasm was coming and I needed that bit more. Then, as if he knew the timing perfectly, he licked me faster and my climax shot up to a new and exquisite height. I had never before felt an orgasm like this and I screamed out loudly. I clutched Michaels buttocks and back and my fingers gouged into his flesh. He gripped my thighs harder and licked me harder and faster. My climax was going on and on and higher and higher. I continued to scream with the pleasure and the passion and Michael went faster and faster and harder and harder. I was out of control, it was frightening, and it seemed the pleasure was going up and up. No orgasm could go on for this long and this intensely. I was crying now, frightened and crying. I felt like I might be trapped into an orgasmic state for the rest of my life. I begged Michael to stop and tried to push him off but I was powerless. The harder I tried, the harder he gripped me, holding me down on the bed and licking my cunt into oblivion. Eventually, it began to subside and with relief I felt in control again. But I could not believe what I had experienced, it was pure pleasure, but so scary. Michael slowly licked me down earth.

He stood up. 'Turn over for me Sarah and kneel on the edge of the bed.'

I did so without question and I watched in the wardrobe mirror as Michaels mighty cock slid inside me. His whole eight inches rammed inside me. He took hold of my hips and he fucked me with the same passion that he licked my cunt with. It was an incredible sight watching yourself being fucked, a huge shaft thrusting inside me and my tits were shaking and banging together.

'Oh god it's beautiful Sarah I can't hold it I'm coming.' Gasped Michael.

I felt his shaft pulsate and felt him coming inside me. I looked in the mirror and as he thrust in and out his cock glistened and dripped with his semen. I had been fucked, well and truly fucked. This young man had made an old lady very very happy.

DESPERATION

I had just dropped Lisa off at school and as I kissed her and made sure she had everything she needed for the day a feeling of guilt and desperation came over me. I waved her farewell from the gate as she merrily skipped into school joined by one of her friends. I returned to the car and was driving home with butterflies in my stomach. I was now a single mum since Bob, my partner had done a runner. He was one of life's losers and whenever he was facing a crisis always took the coward's way out and legged it. We had been together for seven years, which by his standards was a good run, but over the years the cracks started to show. I had taken Sarah with me to stay at my Mother's place for the weekend. Bob didn't like my parents and the feeling was mutual. Lisa and I arrived back late on Sunday afternoon and the house had a sinister feel to it, things seemed to be missing, the TV, the hi-fi. My first reaction was, 'my God, we've been burgled.' Then I saw it; on the table, a note "Sorry Jayne, I can't take anymore, I've got to get out." And that was it, I haven't seen or heard from him since and have no idea where he is. He emptied the joint account and left me with nothing except our daughter, a bad taste in my mouth and a list of debts. Oh the financial institutions were sympathetic enough, but still wanted their money. That was the beginning of my problems; I just couldn't get a job anywhere. I was qualified enough, my typing and computer skills were good and I had a sound knowledge of office accounting systems, but employers these days seem to want to employ kids fresh from school and pay them a pittance. Even my old company, who were noted for paying well, had fallen into this category, they had a new young dynamic production director whose doctrine was "to reduce costs at all costs." Anyway, on with my story.

Today was to be the first day of my new career and I was not looking forward to doing it. I had been driven by desperation to resort to prostitution. I had no real idea of what to do or what to expect, so I had just put an advert in the personal column of the local paper. I must admit I was quite surprised at the response, but I decided that in the beginning, until I knew the ropes, I would limit myself to just two clients today to see how it went. I pulled into the driveway and went in to prepare myself. I decided to wear something simple and easy to remove, so I put on a red checked shirt with the bottom tied in a loose knot that could easily be slipped open. I had it up high to provide some cleavage to show my bust to its best advantage without having a bra to worry about, and left the rest of the buttons undone. It also showed off my midriff. A loose fitting skirt with an elasticised waist band and knickers completed the outfit. Looking at myself in the mirror I must admit for someone approaching thirty, I looked quite good, then sighed and wished that I didn't have to do this. Eventually the neighbours would notice and word would get round, but I was desperate and had a child to feed, so this was the only option at the moment. I sighed and my stomach was turning over with nervousness, it was early in the day, but I needed a drink to calm myself. I went downstairs and poured myself a large vodka and tonic and finished it in a couple of gulps. I had not had any breakfast this morning other than a couple of biscuits and the drink seemed to go straight to my head. I looked at my watch; the first client would be here very soon I thought. Sitting, breathing deeply, I tried to relax. What would the day bring I wondered, what would these men be like, would they be gentlemen, or would they treat me like dirt? My heart leapt as I heard a car door slam. I ran to the window and a man walked down the steps, he was in his mid twenties, tall, handsome and quite distinguished looking. This is it; this must be the first one. I checked my face and hair in the mirror. My heart was pounding. The door knocked and I stifled a scream, I wanted to be anywhere but here. Calm down I thought, you have got to go through with it, think of Lisa. The door knocked again. 'Right, deep breath and go to it.'

I opened the door.

'Hello, I'm Dave.' Said the man with a smile and offering his hand.

'Hi, I'm Jayne, do come in.' I said as I shook his hand.

Well at least he is a gentleman I thought as I directed him to the lounge. I felt slightly more relaxed. 'Can I offer you a drink?' I said and wondered whether prostitutes normally offered their clients a drink.

'No, I won't thank you, I'm driving.'

'Of course, how silly of me. Please take a seat.' I said indicating the settee.

He sat down and put his hands on his knee and I sat beside him and did the same. We both lifted our left arms at the same time to cover a nervous cough. We looked at each other and smiled like a couple of sixteen year olds out on our first date.

'Shall I pay you know?' He enquired.

'Er, well.' And before I could answer he thrust a bundle of cash into my hand. 'Thank you.' I stammered and put the money in my handbag.

'Look, I have to be honest with you,' he blurted, 'I've never done this before.'

'Neither have I.' I said giggling and a little relieved.

'Really.' He replied relaxing visibly.

'Really,' I reassured him. 'We are a couple of virgins then, of sorts.'

'Yes I suppose we are.'

I stood up and took him by the hand. 'Let's go upstairs and loose our virginity together.'

I walked into the bedroom with a lot more confidence than I had ten minutes ago. Dave stood by the door and I stood by the bed. This is it; I thought to myself, I've got to earn my money now. I pushed down the waistband of my skirt and it fell to the floor, Dave sighed as I stood there in my knickers and shirt. I slowly undid the knot and pulled it open and let it slide from my shoulders. My breasts weren't large but they were quite firm and well shaped and I gave them a naughty little wiggle which made Dave's eyes bulge. I gave a girlish giggle and did it again for him. I pushed down my knickers and let them join my skirt. I walked seductively towards Dave, his eyes never leaving my breasts. I took his hands and placed one on each of them. 'Do you like my tits Dave?'

'Oh yes.' He gasped as he caressed them.

'Well they are all yours; you can do whatever you want with them.'

He fell to his knees and sucked and licked them with great passion even trying to get them into his mouth. I felt greatly flattered by his attention and was enjoying it immensely. 'Are you going to take your clothes off?' I whispered to him gently.

He stopped and stood up and almost as an afterthought he realised he was still fully dressed, within a few seconds however, this discrepancy was rectified and he stood naked and erect, very erect. His shaft was a very respectable length, not huge, but very hard and his bulbous end looked very inviting. I went over to the bed and lay down, Dave stood at the foot staring at me. I bent my knees and slowly opened my legs and Dave gasped again. I could feel my pussy was very wet and yearned for attention.

'Well, big boy, fuck me.'

He got onto the bed and kneeled between my thighs, his hands either side of me. He lowered his hips and I reached down and took his shaft and guided it into me. With a gentle thrust I felt his shaft slide in. It had been a long time and the feeling of a hard cock inside me was very pleasant indeed. Dave glided back and forth his shaft invigorating the inside of my cunt, it was beautiful. I reached down and clutched his buttocks and when he was on his upward stroke I pulled him hard and I could feel his cock lurch inside me. He thrust again and I pulled him into me. It was incredibly lovely. Then I thought of the professional game girls who might do this twenty times a day. Would they find it this pleasurable? My thoughts came back to the moment and Dave was thrusting into me with more urgency. Again I assisted his up strokes, pulling his buttocks and his cock slammed hard into my cunt. Dave yelled out in pleasure and I felt his semen shoot inside me like a warm rippling stream. Dave gasped and managed few more valiant thrusts before the energy of his shaft died away.

'That was so incredibly wonderful.' He said breathlessly. 'In fact it was too wonderful and I couldn't hold myself long enough to satisfy you.'

'Don't be silly,' I said, 'it was wonderful and my greatest pleasure, is giving you pleasure.' And I meant that and my thought went back to the professional game girls, surely they don't have twenty orgasms a day.

We both got cleaned up and dressed. My first job was done and it was very enjoyable, made so, I'm sure by Dave. Would the others be like him? As we dressed he told me a little about himself. He worked for his fathers building company as a quantity surveyor, whatever that is, and was as yet still unmarried. He kissed me as I bade him goodbye and I hoped I would see him again. I sighed as I looked at my watch, the next client would be arriving in half an hour. I decided to have a coffee.

Before I got to the kitchen the front door bell rang. Maybe it was Dave returning to ask me to marry him and take me away from all this, I thought wishfully. I opened the door with a hopeful smile to be confronted by a squat ugly man with thick glasses and a suitcase. I had seen him somewhere before but couldn't think where.

'I'm Rupert.' He said with an evil smile.

'You're early.' I stammered, somewhat taken aback by his manner.

'Yes, I wanted to catch you while you were still warm from your last client.' He said with a sinister tone to his voice.

He then walked in, rudely brushing me aside. I felt bad vibes straight away and like a fool I closed the front door and followed him in. My first instinct was to run after Dave, I was later to regret not following my instinct. I decided in my mind that this profession was not for me, there was no way I could have sex with a man like this, no matter what he paid me. 'Look,' I said, 'I'm afraid I'm going to have to cancel our appointment, an emergency has cropped up'.

He turned to face me, without speaking. He had a very pale complexion with dark thick stubble on his face. His hair jet black and greasy and around his tight collar body hair protruded. He made me cringe. He removed his glasses and wiped them with a filthy handkerchief, replaced them to cover his beady black eyes and gave me the same sinister grin he gave me at the door.

'Cancel our appointment! Oh no my dear it doesn't work like that.'

His tone chilled my blood; I needed to get rid of this evil man. 'Look,

I must ask you to leave.' I said desperately and putting my hand on his shoulder to usher him out.

'No.' He said aggressively and swept my arm aside with a swing of his left arm and on the return swing his arm swung back and the back of his huge hairy hand hit me full in the face. I banged my head as I fell and I must have passed out. The nightmare had begun.

I regained consciousness, my face hurt and my head was throbbing. I was in the bedroom sitting in the bedside chair; I was confused and disorientated and couldn't tell how much time had passed. Then it all started coming back to me and I remembered where I had seen this creep before, it was at the theatre. Not that I'm a big theatre goer but the play that was showing was an evil piece. I didn't want to go to see it because it had a reputation for being highly sexually explicit and had a particularly gruesome ending that was reported to have made members of the audience sick. The boyfriend I was with then, relished that kind of thing, but even that was too much for him and he too was sick. As he was throwing up in the gutter outside, this hideous monster came shuffling out of the theatre sniggering and cackling like a madman. That madman was now in my house. As my vision slowly cleared, the evil monster was sitting on the bed playing with something metallic. I caught my reflection in the dressing table mirror and I couldn't believe my eyes, I had a gash above my eye and a trickle of blood down my cheek and my nose was swollen and bleeding and I could taste the blood on my lips. But what shocked me the most was that I was naked and bound. This creep had undressed me and tied me up. My hands were behind my back, my wrists in leather straps with a ten inch length of chain connecting them. There was a two foot metal bar between my thighs secured by leather straps just above my knee, so I was sitting naked with my legs open with this pervert looking up my crutch. But the worst indignity was a two inch wide studded dog collar around my neck with a chain coming from it and the chain was fastened to a clasp in the middle of the bar, so I was unable to stand up straight. I was soon to find out that this binding had a more sinister application.

'Feeling better my dear?' He sneered.

'You bastard, untie me.' I snapped.

'I think not.'

'I'll scream the place down.'

'Please do. In fact I insist. No one will hear you, your neighbours are all at work and I see you have had the good sense to install double glazing, very considerate of you.'

'What do you want from me?'

'I want to hurt you; I want you to suffer exquisite agony.'

'Why?'

'It's my greatest pleasure, pure and simple, and I haven't been able to indulge myself for some years. I've been in prison you see. My last little escapade went wrong. Not really my fault you understand. She was alive when I left, in agony but alive. I left the manacles on as a thank you present because she had screamed louder than anyone else that I had previously entertained. Silly woman, she tried to get out and fell down the stairs and broke her back. She lay alone in agony and died of thirst days later. I wish I'd known, I could have visited her every day and tormented her. They found me eventually though, but they couldn't keep me in prison forever, so here I am. The beautiful thing is my dear, is that it's not my fault, I have this unusual genetic problem with an unpronounceable name and basically my sexual prowess is somewhat exaggerated, as is my lust for inflicting pain. I have a huge penis you know, twelve inches long and three inches thick. You will enjoy that later, but that is the only thing you will enjoy, the rest of the enjoyment will be mine alone.'

I felt cold fear come over me, I am going to die this afternoon, die a horrible agonising death at the hands of this brute. I immediately thought of Lisa, she would be waiting for me, I felt like crying. He stood up and I heard metallic objects jangle on the bed.

'Oh I haven't shown you my toys yet have I.' He said picking up a pair of gardener's secateurs. 'Look at these, very useful for pruning the roses but,' and his voice lowered, 'equally good for snipping off ears and nipples. And this, a bow saw with large jagged rusty teeth, so much more agonising and messy for cutting off breasts, than a knife. And finally this.'

He picked up something that looked like a large tuning fork.

'This is one of my favourites, put it in a fire until its red hot then plunge it into your eyes. Lovely, your eyeballs bubble out like fried eggs.'

His graphic descriptions made me feel physically sick.

'But some light entertainment first I think.' He said throwing down the tuning fork that clanked onto the other metal objects.

He took off his clothes and what an obscene sight he was. He was incredibly muscular but he was also very very hairy. His whole body was covered and he looked like a Neanderthal. Even his penis had hair along its length and he didn't exaggerate about its size, it was monstrous, with a huge purple bell end the size of tennis ball. There was no way any woman would comfortably take that length. He strode over to me and picked me up roughly, the dog collar wrenching my neck. Then throwing me unceremoniously onto the bed, turning me over and pulling my ankles so I was kneeling on the edge of the bed, my hands behind my back and the collar gouging into my neck. It was unbelievably uncomfortably and as he dragged me I left a trail of blood on the bed from my still bleeding wounds. He rummaged through his instruments of torture and picked out a bullwhip and I just prayed to God for mercy and thought of Lisa. I saw him in the mirror and he lifted his arm ready for the first lash. The whip hit a vase on the window sill and sent it crashing down onto the patio below.

'Oh dear these modern houses are so small there isn't room to swing a whip.' He said closing the window. 'There you can scream as load as you like now.' He said with an evil sneer. He threw his bullwhip into his bag and pulled out a riding crop.

'I'll have to make do with this I suppose.' He sighed, with an air of disappointment.

He raised his arm above his head and I could see the look of extreme effort in the mirror as the whip whistled through the air. With an agonising burning sting it hit my buttocks. I screamed out with the pain.

'That's it my dear, scream out loud, I like it when they scream, it makes my cock harder.'

He raised his arm again, and again the whip whistled through the air and burnt into my tender flesh, once more I screamed in agony. It was unbearable. The pain, the discomfort of his cruel bindings, the thought of never seeing my little Lisa again was too much to bear. I felt hopeless;

there was no way out of this living nightmare. My thoughts were jolted by another stroke of his lash on my tortured flesh. I screamed again and this sadistic bastard laughed a maniacal cackle like an horrendous witch. I hated and feared this monster. How long would this go on for? I thought of his last poor victim who he left to die in agony and his pleasure and disappointment that he missed an opportunity to make her days of agonising death more painful. Then my stomach turned as I thought of those big jagged teeth on his bow saw and his sick pleasure of hacking off my breasts with it. I just couldn't stand that. Once again the whip gouged into my flesh and I screamed and cried with the pain and the hopelessness of the situation, but my overriding concern was for my daughter. And again the whip whistled through the air and burnt into me. My buttocks were just a burning agony and my body twitched all over with the excruciating pain. Then mercifully he paused in his flogging, I took a deep breath. I knew my agony wasn't over, but I was glad of the break. As I knelt there, bound and powerless I felt trickles of blood running down the back of my thighs and my mind thought about what his next sick pleasure was going to be. My head and face were still throbbing from his first assault and as I kneeled with my neck aching and my head to on side on the bed, he walked into my eye line with his huge cock in his hand, rubbing its length with sick pride.

'Now for some sex fun my dear.' He said, his beady black eyes glowing with pleasure behind his thick glasses. 'A little lubrication is in order I think.' And with that he leaned over me to reach into his bag and I cringed as his filthy cock touched my face as he did so. He reached out a tube of lubricating jelly and squirted a pool of it into his palm and he slowly rubbed his entire length with it. He cackled to himself as the pervert went behind me. I watched in the mirror as he got into position then I closed my eyes. He was going to brutally rape me and I just couldn't bear to watch. I felt his huge cock positioning itself; it was nuzzling my vulva. I felt his rough hairy hands grasping my hips and I could feel his rancid breath on my back. I braced myself for the inevitable, I screwed my eyes tight shut and cried and prayed.

There was a crash of things falling over, a dull thud, a gasp and another thud. What was he going to do to me? He had released my hips. I opened my eyes and the monster was crawling on the floor, he had lost his glasses. Then another thud and he slumped to the floor.

'Dave.' I howled in unbelievable relief.

He quickly reached into the monsters bag and produced a pair of handcuffs and manacled the monster to the leg of the bed. I broke down in an uncontrollable welter of tears. Dave had saved my life.

'This creep passed me on your driveway as I was leaving. He brushed passed me without speaking. I drove away but couldn't help think the worst, so I had to turn around and come back.'

'Oh Dave I can't tell you how grateful I am.' I said still crying. Dave released me from the bindings.' But how did you get in?'

'You left the back door unlocked. My suspicions were confirmed when I found the broken vase on the patio.'

The police were called and Rupert was taken away. The nightmare was over.

A few days later I was recovering at home and the door bell rang. Dave stood there with a huge bouquet of flowers. Again I just broke down in tears as soon as I saw him. We went into the living room and he took me in his arms and kissed me passionately.

'You've got that skirt on again.' He said.

'Just coincidence.' I replied.

Within seconds Dave was completely naked. He pulled down my skirt and my knickers and sat me on the settee. He kneeled down and parted my legs and pushed me back. He kissed the inside of my thigh, getting slowly higher. 'Take me Dave.' He reached my passion slit and gently kissed it; I reached down and parted my soft, moist, yearning flesh for him. Dave moaned with pleasure as he accepted the invitation. His tongue slid deeply and easily into my juicy little cunt. It made me shiver all over with pleasure. I gasped in rapture. I pulled my cunt open wider and upwards, so my clitoris was exposed for his attention. Again he needed no further encouragement and Dave expertly licked my clit to exquisite pleasure. I wanted him so much. He licked my clitoris so expertly; he knew exactly what I wanted and how I wanted it. I could feel myself on the brink of orgasm. I needed just a little more to take me into space. That final lick took over me and my body was overwhelmed with orgasm. I screamed out with pleasure. Dave licked harder; I grasped his head forcing his tongue onto my clitty I wanted to pull him into my cunt. I was out of control with explosive orgasm and I screamed out loudly with the pleasure of it all. Eventually I reached the plateau and Dave timed it perfectly. He gave my clit one last suck and took his cock and let it find its way into my tunnel of love. With one mighty thrust it sank deeply inside me. He thrust like a demon and I felt it reach the top of my cunt. I had come but I wanted more, I wanted Dave to fill my cunt with his hot semen. I didn't have to wait long, he gasped and cried out. I felt his cock throbbing inside me and with a mighty yell his semen shot inside me. Dave thrust on and I heard it squelching inside and felt it oozing out of my cunt and running down my thighs. What a performance.

'I owed you an orgasm.' He said afterwards.

'And I owe you this.' I replied.

'What's this for?'

'It's the money you paid me. I decided not to pursue that career.'

'I'm glad. In fact I would like you to come and work for me.' He said.

And that is what I did. Corny as it sounds, my life, our life is on track and we have a rewarding relationship. Rupert has been put away for life and all is well with the world.

THE DECORATORS

D ecorating, as with all things DIY, seemed to be a no go area with Darren. Its not that he was lazy, it's just I could never get him motivated to do anything. The only thing he showed any interest in was the garden and he showered lots of love and affection on it. I have to admit it looked good and always caused glances of admiration from passers by. The interior of the house however, was not a reflection of the outside vista; in fact I was almost ashamed to invite anyone inside because of the poor state of the décor. Perhaps, poor state, would be something of an understatement, the living room was a shambles. My main point of concern was the area on the chimney breast above the fireplace. Two years ago we had the original gas fire replaced with a simulated flame fire, which I have to say looked very good. The problem was that it seemed to send a higher percentage of its heat up the flu than the old one did and consequently the chimney breast became very warm causing the wallpaper to split. So we had an eighteen inch fissure in the wallpaper that ran up from the mantelpiece, we did have a mirror on the wall that covered most of it, but the worst bit was the first six inches and the wallpaper being thick and patterned made it look all the worse. Plus the feature fireplace being the focal point of the room, the eye was inevitably drawn to this hideous crevasse in the wallpaper. It was so embarrassing, everyone who visited always looked at it, then at me, with a pitiful look in their eye as if to say "Poor woman, fancy having to live in a dump like this, what must your husband be like?"

Some time ago I had a holiday brochure delivered which I always kept at the side of the hi-fi, so if we were expecting visitors I would place it over the split. The ploy was not always successful, because people would see it and think "Oh, cruise holidays in the Arctic, I've always fancied that." They would then pick it up and I would cringe with embarrassment as they silently stared at this great rift in the paper. They always quickly replaced the brochure without further comment about the Arctic and its manifold pleasures and I would always mutter some claim about the fact that decorating was due to start tomorrow. That excuse was wearing thin and I was adamant that something was going to be done. I had badgered Darren about it for months and it was always the same excuse, "Well you know I'm no good at papering." Well I was determined that the job was going to be done, so we reached a compromise, we would strip the old wallpaper off and do any preparation work that was necessary, then we would get a professional decorator in to hang the paper. The plan was agreed, and just to ensure that Darren was motivated into action I had installed the proviso that there would be no sex for him until his part of the project was complete. My legs would remain closed henceforth and if he required sexual satisfaction he would have to depend on a good memory and a good right hand. The stipulation had the desired effect and Darren was galvanised into action and fulfilled his part of the bargain with gusto and a permanent hard on.

We had contacted a decorating company that was recommended by someone who worked with Darren, "Phil and Les, Decorators of Distinction" was how their business card was headed and underneath it said "Satisfaction Guaranteed" So as they were recommended, we engaged them. We were up early and the weather forecast was good, so we completely emptied the living room onto the patio giving the decorators the maximum room to work in. Darren was going to take the car to Pete's, a friend of his, to have it serviced, so I was left to supervise the decorators.

At nine thirty, exactly as arranged a white van with ladders and boards on the top pulled up outside. Well at least they were punctual and in my mind's eye I had a preconceived vision of what they would be like. I thought there would be a flash one, who would be the boss and he would get out of the van and flick his cigarette end into the road. The other would be short, fat and not too clever looking and get out of the van scratching his balls. They would both be scruffy and unshaven and have an old paint splashed radio that would be loud and badly tuned to some inane station that ought to be called Radio Mindless. I went through to the kitchen to switch on the kettle; these tradesmen usually can't start work until they have had a cup of something. As I switched it on the door bell rang. I bustled through to let them in. On opening the door the first thing I saw was the ubiquitous radio. It was in a clear plastic bag so was not the paint speckled mess I had predicted. In fact in the ensuing few seconds all my pre judgements were to be dispelled. The radio was being held in a pair of very delicate white hands with manicured nails. As my eyes slowly travelled upwards I was treated to a vision of beauty in a figure hugging boiler suit that was unzipped enough to reveal a huge plunging cleavage and nipples sticking out like fifteen millimetre rivets. Instead of two sweaty uncouth men, I was presented with two beautiful women. The one holding the radio had short red hair with a wispy fringe and beautiful pale ivory skin. Her partner was similarly dressed, had dark hair that was just above shoulder length and cut so it curled around her jaw and she had a full fringe. She was thicker set than the other with an even larger bust, which her boiler suit seemed to be having difficulty in containing. By contrast she had darker features with beautiful hazel eyes and a delicate light tan.

'Hi, we're Phil and Les.' Said the red head.

'Oh right,' I burbled somewhat taken aback, 'I just thought...'

'The names! Yes it always surprises people. We did it like that on purpose; it sounds more tradesmen like than Phillipa and Lesley.' Said the dark haired one.

'Well I'm Jean, no confusion there.' I replied.

'Unless you're French.' Said the red head, with a giggle.

'Unless you're French.' I reiterated. 'Er which is...?' I asked.

'I'm Phillipa.' Said the red head.

'And I'm Lesley.'

'Right well come in.'

We all entered the lounge and they gave the room a once over with a professional eye.

'You've made a good job of the prepping.' Said Phil. 'Shouldn't take too long to get the paper up.'

'There's the paper.' I said indicating a pyramid of rolls in the corner. 'I hope I've estimated it correctly.'

Phil picked up a roll and unfurled a length. 'Yes, a simple pattern, shouldn't be too difficult to match up. Should be plenty there, I think. In fact any unstarted rolls you may be able to take back.'

'I'll get the stuff in.' Said Les.

'Would you both like coffee?'

'Black no sugar for me please.' Said Les, as she went out to the van.

'And for you?' I asked Phil.

'Oh white with one sugar please.' She said in a very slow sultry voice fixing my gaze with her beautiful pale green eyes.

I found I was transfixed by her gaze and felt a kind of energy from her. She rolled up the roll of paper and seductively let her hand grasp it and slowly slide up and down its length. Her gaze then transferred to the shaft of paper in her hand as she continued to stroke its length. Momentarily I caught her questioning gaze, then her eyes travelled down and I could feel them caressing my breasts. I looked down and I could see my nipples becoming erect and showing through my T-shirt. I was also aware of a strange tingling and my face beginning to flush. Les entered with an armful of equipment. She saw my blushing face and I saw her eyes momentarily dip to examine my erect nipples. She gave a knowing smile and I felt my face getting redder. 'I'll just get the coffee.' I coughed, and exited to the kitchen to compose myself. As I left I heard them both give a girlish giggle.

I prepared the coffee. My hands were trembling; thoughts were racing through my mind. Visions of long ago and memories of Lisa, I had tried to suppress the memories, now they had surfaced again.

'Can I have a bucket of water?'

'Oh.' I squeaked in terror.

'I'm sorry; I didn't mean to startle you.' Apologised Les.

'Its alright, I was miles away.' I gasped with my hand on my chest.

Les filled her bucket from the sink and as she turned I was still breathing heavily. She put down her bucket and approached, taking my shoulders to reassure me. 'Relax; let nature take its course.' She said in a soft comforting way.

I felt at ease and I rubbed her forearm gently with the palm of my hand. Her boiler suit, like Phil's was unzipped by an indecent amount and her large heaving bosom filled my vision. She knew I was being drawn into it. She put her finger under my chin and lifted my head and slowly leaned towards me placing a delicate warm kiss on my lips. Our eyes were locked for a few seconds.

'Work to be done.' She said gently pulling away. 'Business before pleasure.'

Les picked up her bucket of water and disappeared into the lounge. I continued with the coffee, my hands still trembling and my mind full of confused emotions.

Work was in full swing when I entered the lounge with the coffee. Phil was halfway up her step ladder smoothing out the wallpaper and as she reached up the fabric of the boiler suit seemed to be stretched to bursting point. Her hips were at face height and I couldn't help but notice her pubic mound. The material was so sheer and clinging it showed her every contour as if she was naked, the crutch of her boiler suit went between her pussy lips and I could clearly see their outline. If I had looked more closely I felt sure I would be able to see the outline of her clitoris. They both paused momentarily to acknowledge the coffee. Again I felt this amorous electricity from them both. It excited and confused me and I didn't know what to do. Deciding I needed a breathing space I made an excuse to get out. I would go to the shop on some pretext and hoped by the time I returned Darren would be back so my dilemma would be over. 'I'm just going to pop down to the shop, we're a bit low on milk and bread, can I get either of you anything?'

'A packet of chocolate biscuits would be nice.' Replied Les.

'More biscuits,' interjected Phil, 'don't you think your tits are big enough.'

'You're just jealous.' Said Les with a giggle.

'There's no need to be jealous, I think your bust is more than ample.' I said, and I could have bitten my tongue off for saying it.

'Well thank you Jean, that's very nice of you to say so.' She said, giving me that knowing smile.

I felt my face flushing again so I made a hasty exit to catch my breath and think things over.

I made the shopping trip last as long as possible and as I walked down the street my heart skipped a beat as Darren's car still wasn't there. 'Only me I shouted as I entered.'

'Hi.' Came the reply.

I was amazed at the progress they had made in that short time, in fact the job was almost done. 'My word you have done well.'

'Just one more should do it.' Said Les as she passed the last piece of pasted wallpaper to Phil waiting on the stepladder.

She carefully positioned it and it slid into place exactly. A few smoothing strokes with her wallpaper brush and the job was done.

'Finito.' Said Phil in triumph.

I inspected the job and was most impressed. 'That is excellent, well done and it's taken hardly any time at all. It would have taken Darren half a week to do that, assuming of course if he ever got up steam to do such a job, which is unlikely.'

Phil brushed off a few trimmings of wallpaper that clung to her bust with her finger tips and I couldn't help but watch as she did it. It felt almost as though she was doing it for my benefit. She caught my eye and smiled and continued to brush her breasts even though the offending debris had been removed. Her nipples became erect and protruded invitingly through the fabric of her suit. I felt this time that I was going to go with the flow. 'Nice figure Phil.' I croaked.

'Thank you.'

And she let her hands flow over her breasts, down her side and over her hips to her thighs.

'Er shall I wait in the van?' Enquired Les.

'No. Please stay.' I said positively. I had decided in my mind to open the emotional and sexual floodgates. Phil slowly unzipped her suit to the navel; she pulled it apart and let her breasts free. They were beautifully firm and round and the texture of her skin was like ivory silk, contrasting wonderfully with her cherry red nipples.

'Take them.' She said and I slowly reached out to caress them. They were so warm and inviting, I caressed them lovingly in my trembling hands. Phil put her hands on mine and pulled them onto her breasts and tilting her head back, sighed with sexual emotion. I felt Les's hands on my waist and standing behind me she slowly lifted my t-shirt. Letting go of Phil's breasts, they wobbled gently as they were released and I raised my arms to let Les lift off my t-shirt. Waves of excitement flowed over me, my nipples were erect and my cunt was wet and tingling for attention. Phil brushed her suit from her shoulders and her breasts wobbled erotically as she shuffled to free her shoulders. She peeled it down her waist and over her hips and I gasped as I saw she was wearing no knickers. Her pubic mound was wonderful and the flesh of her vulva was full, rounded and very inviting. She bent forward as she slid the garment down her white thighs and legs, kicking it free along with her trainers. She was naked and beautiful and she was mine. I stood there taking in her beauty and Les unclipped my bra and gently pushed the straps from my shoulder letting it fall away. I shuffled my shoulders to make my tits shake. Phil gasped in approval. They weren't as nice as hers and although they were quite large, they sagged. I fondled my own breasts and let out a sigh, then caressed them erotically as she had done earlier. Again she gasped and she slid her hand slowly down her belly to her pussy. Her middle finger followed the line of her labia and I heard the gentle squelch of her wetness and her gasp of pleasure as her finger parted her lips and found her clitoris.

Les had unzipped my jeans and was sliding them down, along with my knickers. I lifted my feet in turn to let her undress me. I turned to face her and I took her zip and slowly pulled it down, her huge tits were aching to get out and I was aching to see them. Sliding my hands gently inside and across her shoulders I pushed the suit from her and down her arms. Her breasts were huge. Les was very broad shouldered and in turn her breasts were big and wide in perfect proportion. Although a very robust woman, she had a very narrow waist and with her wide hips she had a very attractive hour glass figure. She shook her arms free of the sleeves and it made her tits bounce about for me. I quickly whipped off her suit and the three of us stood naked. Les took me in her arms and I felt her huge tits pressing into mine. She kissed me passionately and as she did so I felt Phil's hands messaging my buttocks. It was magical, it was the stuff of dreams, the stuff of fantasy, I was receiving the attention of two women. Les continued to kiss me, then I felt her hand take my breast, I sighed with pleasure. Phil's hands were on my back and she kissed me between my shoulder blades then slowly let her lips and her hands get lower until she reached my buttocks. She caressed and kneaded them, pulling them apart and kissing and gently biting them. It was wonderful. Les began sucking my tits and I screamed out with pleasure as I felt Phil's fingers slide between my lips and stroke my clitoris. It was brilliant and I was drunk with sexual pleasure

Phil pulled back the dust sheet they had laid over the carpet and automatically I went and lay down. She then opened a holdall and took out an enormous vibrator. It was about ten inches long and was a perfect, better than perfect replica of a penis; it even had veins and testicles. Then she took out a small thermos flask and emptied the contents into the base. 'What's that?' I asked.

'Warm milk,' she replied, 'when you come you squeeze the balls and it ejaculates into you.'

I was getting very excited; the vibrator had an exaggerated bulbous end, the rim of which was studded with soft rubber nodules. I opened my legs and raised my knees. Les's knees were either side of my head. 'Lick me.' She begged,

I happily obliged and guided her hips down so that her clitoris was in reach. She squealed in delight as my tongue slowly stroked her. I felt the vibrator nuzzling up to my pussy lips and I could feel it slowly sliding into me. It was the biggest thing I had ever had inside me and I shivered with excitement. Phil turned the vibrator on and it sent me sky high, it vibrated against my clit and made the inside of my cunt tingle like nothing else before. On and on it slid, it felt unbelievably tight and I could feel it stretching me, any bigger and it would split me open. She pushed it hard and it reached the end of my cunt, I screamed partly in pain and partly in pleasure. Phil knew my capacity and gauged it beautifully and rapidly thrust the vibrator in and out of me. The rubber nodules on the rim of the knob end rubbed and vibrated against my g-spot sending me into ecstasy.

Meanwhile I was licking Les and she was getting near to orgasm. She was pressing her cunt hard down onto my mouth and I kept my tongue rigid as she just gyrated her cunt back and forth over my mouth. She was riding me like a wild stallion and was crying with ecstasy. She gripped my tits and was pulling herself down hard onto me. I arched my back, my tits were being pulled so hard I thought she would rip them off. My cunt was being stretched like never before and all the time Les was grinding her cunt into my mouth. I was in pain and rapturous ecstasy and I wanted more. Phil pumped the vibrator harder into me, ramming me faster and faster. I still wanted more. I reached down and started to finger my clitoris bringing me on faster. Phil squealed with delight as she saw me doing it.

'You too, gasped Les, 'you finger yourself.

I then heard Phil squeal again and it turned me on knowing she was fingering herself as well. She was obviously very worked up as I heard her scream in orgasm very quickly. Seconds later Les pulled hard onto my tits and ground her clit into my mouth and exploded into orgasm. Throughout her orgasm Phil kept ramming me with the vibrator and I felt myself coming. Les had lifted herself off my face and I was free to scream out my orgasm, which I did and Phil with perfect timing squeezed the balls of the vibrator sending a wave of warm milk gushing into my cunt. It was fantastically realistic and the pseudo semen squelched out of me in great gushes. What an unbelievable experience.

We got cleaned up and dressed and everything was cleared away. They got in their van and drove away just as Darren returned with the car.

'How were they?' Enquired Darren.

'Brilliant, I replied, I've asked them to come and do the kitchen next week.

RINGING SWINGING
BONDAGE BENCH

∞

I lay in bed listening to the gentle tick of the clock as Dave lay asleep and gently snoring beside me. I could see by the glow through the curtains that the sun was shining. A feeling of bliss and contentment flowed over me, it was Saturday morning and the weekend lay ahead. A leisurely day in the garden, I thought to myself and tonight, to Sheila and Ted's for a barbeque and swingers evening. We have had some very raunchy sessions at Sheila and Ted's and it made me feel horny just thinking about it. Dave rolled over onto his back still snoring gently and I noticed from the tent in the bed that he had a hard on. It has always fascinated me why men always seem to have erections when they are asleep, maybe erotic dreams I thought, but he always denied that, a denial I always found hard to believe. I decided to have a bit of fun and maybe try to interact with his dream, so I gently peeled back the sheets and there it was, two pounds of throbbing, pulsating, ramrod stiff, cock. I looked at it, gently bobbing in time with his pulse. I sighed to myself as I thought of the many hours of pleasure it had given and been given over the years. His huge cock end stood proud of the shaft, the rim of which, in my mind I could almost feel inside my tunnel of love, rubbing my inside to exquisite pleasures. I shivered at the beautiful thought.

Dave was obviously still fast asleep and I kneeled beside him and let my breasts dangle over his shaft, letting each one stroke and tantalize it.

120

I teased his end with my nipple letting it touch his hole which a small bead of semen was seeping out and as I pulled away it formed a fine strand. Dave moaned in his sleep, I was obviously becoming part of his dream. I went down on him and took his shaft end in my mouth, I had to really open my mouth to get it in and his bell end was all I could take comfortably. As I sucked his huge purple end my hand went to work on his shaft, gently rubbing and caressing its length. Dave moaned and shuffled, I was obviously stimulating him greatly. My hand continued to work him and my tongue lapped the end of his cock, I felt the salty taste of his seeping semen and I sucked it from him. It gave me a thrill and I tried to take his cock deeper into my mouth trying to make him think he was fucking me, sliding gently in and out of my tight little cunt. I took it in and out of my mouth and rubbed his shaft with the same rhythm so it felt that I was astride him lowering myself onto his shaft then lifting up and sucking him, then sinking down deeply on him again. I kept this going until I could feel him coming. His breathing became deeper and I could feel his shaft pulsating, I stopped sucking him and kept working him with my hand. I dangled my tits in front of his cock and with a mighty roar he shot his load all over me. My tits were covered with strands of semen and I squeezed out every last drop onto them. Poor Dave began to wake up and was completely disorientated, he didn't know whether he had a wet dream or if it was real. I lay back on the bed beside him with my hands behind my head showing off my tits all covered with his semen. Dave shuffled up onto his elbows and saw my semen covered tits then looked down at his dripping cock.

'You naughty girl.' He said with a gleam in his eye.

Up until lunchtime Dave was busy in his workshop putting the finishing touches to his latest secret project. I was about to prepare the meal when I heard a clatter that sounded like falling scaffolding coming from the living room. I dashed in thinking something had hit the house and on the floor was a pile of black metal tubing, chains, and boards of various sizes with padded black vinyl surfaces and other miscellaneous bits and pieces. Dave came in with another armful of similar things and dropped it with the rest.

'What's all this rubbish?' I enquired.

'Lucy, feast your eyes on my latest invention.' He replied enthusiastically. 'The ultimate sex aid, the ringing swinging bondage bench.'

'Looks like a pile of scrap to me.'

'It's a flat pack, it needs assembling.'

'I see.' I said, not really interested, thinking that it resembled a dismantled weight training device that you see in the gym. 'What's it for?'

'Well it's obvious, isn't it? Its going to revolutionise people's sex lives.' He said with great confidence.

I was all for a sexual revolution, but I must admit I couldn't visualise how this pile of rubbish was going to achieve it.

'And tonight is going to be its world premiere.' He announced as if it was the latest block buster movie.

'Tonight?'

'Yes, at Ted and Sheila's bash.'

'But all they'll be interested in is burgers, steak and sex. Ted and Sheila won't want all this stuff lying about.' I protested.

'But it's all arranged, they are both very enthusiastic. I told Ted what it can be used for and they are both really keen to try it out. I'm going round with it now to set it up, so when everyone has eaten their food and ready for a bit of action, it will be unveiled and ready to go.'

'Mmm.' I said somewhat unsold on the idea.

'Have faith, it will suit every sexual orientation. They will be fighting to get to try it.'

I helped Dave to load it into the car and off he went to Ted's place to set it up. I have to admit as the afternoon went on I kept thinking about this contraption and all those chains manacles and some sort of sling and wondered how they would work. We had indulged in a bit of bondage in the past and indeed some of our swinger friends were deeply into it. So there might be something in it, after all if Ted was interested, it might be an eventful evening.

Dave returned in a couple of hours with a big smile on his face.

'All set and working perfectly.' He said with great enthusiasm.

We had a nap in the afternoon to ready ourselves for this evening's extravaganza, which going by previous experience, can be an enjoyable but exhausting event.

That evening we drove into the sweeping driveway of Ted and Sheila's at about seven thirty, there were quite a few cars already there, ones that we knew, the old crowd and a few unfamiliar ones. It would be a mix of the old reliables and the fresh and exciting. I always felt excited at this point, a feeling of nervousness and adventure, but I knew after a couple of drinks I would be surveying the prey. How many cocks would I get inside me tonight I wondered? Dave parked the car next to Ted's Merc and we rang the bell. I dressed simply and tartly, short, tight black skirt, red stilettos and an old checked lumberjack shirt, sleeves rolled up to just below the elbows and the bottom tied to show my bare midriff. No bra, partly to save time undressing and partly to let my tits swing free beneath this voluminous shirt which would keep male, and maybe some female attention, plus my tits moving against the fabric would keep my nipples permanently erect. And no tights of course, I have never seen anyone elegantly get out of tights. On the other hand, panties can be removed with a gentle bow to seductively dangle the tits, a little push with the thumbs or fingers, then gravity usually does the rest. I could feel my pussy tingle and become moist just thinking about it. Sheila opened the door wearing just one of Ted's old white shirts and blue knickers. The material was almost transparent and her huge breasts and nipples could easily be seen underneath.

'Like the outfit Sheila.' Said Dave.

'Do you love,' she replied looking down at herself, 'its just one of Ted's old ones, he wants to rip it off me and ravish me on your machine later, so I couldn't put a good one on.'

We went in and mingled, had a few drinks and nibbles and were introduced to a few newcomers, one of which really tickled my fancy. 'This is Roger,' said Sheila, 'it's his first time so maybe you could show him the ropes, as it were.'

'Show him the ropes.' I repeated. 'Sheila's little joke.'

'I'm sorry?' Said Roger, a little confused.

'Ropes. Sheila and Ted are into bondage.

'Oh I see.' Said Roger a little nervously. 'You'll have to excuse me, I'm a bit green.'

'Stick with me kid and we'll soon have you up to speed.' I said eyeing him up and down as I sipped my gin and tonic. I had to admit he was a fine looking specimen. Tall with dark thick hair brushed back. He was wearing a figure hugging short sleeved white shirt that showed his physique to perfection. He was very athletic looking without being over muscular and had a firm square jaw and brown eyes. His black slacks were also a snug fit and as I pretended to adjust the knot of my shirt I inspected the outline of his sexual apparatus which seemed very ample. The cut of his trousers seemed to lift and support his balls and a huge sausage of a cock lay pointing to the left above them. It looked a good four inches on the slack and very fat. I made a promise to myself that tonight I would see it in its full splendid erect state and also feel it shoot its load inside me. I was visualising its size when Sheila intervened and swept him away.

'Don't hog him all to yourself dear.' Announced Sheila. 'People are asking to be introduced.'

With that he was dragged backwards into the crowd. I had a few more drinks and mingled with the others, but I could not get Roger out of my mind. Just then Gemma came over. I hadn't seen her at our swinger's parties for a few months. She was a bubbly vivacious bundle of fun was Gemma and very much into nature and hippy culture. Obviously in the party mood as all she was wearing was one of her usual colorful rag skirts and sandals. Completely topless except for layers of bead necklaces and her long hair and as she skipped towards me her huge breasts shook and wobbled completely out of control. She was in her mid forties and over a quarter of a century without a bra had done her no favors as they sagged nearly to her waist. Having said that, they were very big and certainly caught the eye. I recalled one memorable evening when under the influence of certain substances she was astride her current boyfriend, fucking him savagely and her huge tits bounced about unbelievably, almost smacking her in the face. The intensity of her passion was so great everyone stood and watched. They were partly fascinated by the animation of her tits and also the intensity of the grinding of her hips on her poor boyfriend's cock and we all hoped she would climax before she snapped his appendage off. Anyway she was bouncing and steaming towards me in a much exited state, waving her arms and her tits at me.

'Oh Lucy, she said excitedly, 'how nice to see you again.'

'Gemma.' I said kissing her and playfully squeezing her tits. Gemma liked it both ways.

'I've started the summer of love.' She said enthusiastically.

'I think it's been done.' I replied.

'Not like I do it.' She said. 'I've invented the cart wheel.'

'That's also been done.' I added.

'Not like mine.' She said with a big smile on her face.

I had to admit I was puzzled.

'But,' she continued, 'I've invented something even better than the cartwheel; the Catherine wheel.'

'The what?'

'The Catherine wheel, you know the pin wheel, the spiral firework that spins.'

I began to wonder if she was under the influence of some exotic intoxicant or other, as she certainly wasn't making herself very clear. After all fireworks and cart wheels had been around for centuries.

'It's a sexual revolution. We started with the cart wheel, but that wasn't a very efficient use of space, but by jingo the Catherine wheel is going to be the greatest thing since sliced bread.'

She was obviously so excited with this project that she was not explaining herself properly. She probably had a clear vision in her mind put wasn't putting it across properly to the layman. 'Gemma, calm down and explain to me simply about your invention of the cart wheel.'

She took a swig of her wine and her tits applauded in gratification. 'Well, it's like this, have you ever done sixty nines on your side?'

'Well, no, I've always done it on top of someone or someone on top of me.'

'Right well for this exercise imagine doing it on your side.' She explained.

'Got that.' I said.

'Now as you are sucking Dave's cock, and instead of Dave licking your clitoris, imagine you are the other way round and someone else doing it.'

My quim was getting wet with the thought.

'Then,' continued Gemma, 'imagine someone else sucking his cock and Dave licking her clitoris. So you see, you have a cartwheel of four people alternatively facing opposite directions, giving each other oral sex.'

'Brilliant.' I shouted. 'Simple but brilliant.'

'And the beauty of it is that any number of people can participate, and they don't have to be straight; they can be same sex partners. The disadvantage is however, the more people there are, the bigger the wheel, but at last years festival we did it in a meadow.'

'That is amazing.' I said. 'I'm really impressed.'

'The most exciting thing is going to be this year's festival; we are going to do the Catherine wheel.'

'And what's that?'

'Basically very similar principle but with a more efficient use of space. With the Cartwheel, it just becomes a bigger circle with nothing in the middle. The Catherine wheel is a spiral that starts with one person in the middle being sucked or licked by their partner then it expands onto the next one in a tightly packed spiral. The advantage is you can get more bodies into a smaller space than with the cart wheel. The disadvantage is that the first one at the centre of the spiral is getting but not giving and the last one on the outside edge is giving but not getting, but we will arrange for them to meet up afterwards so that everyone is satisfied.'

I sighed at the thought of hundreds, possibly thousands of people having oral sex at the same time but Gemma had obviously given this project a lot of thought and had big plans, as she went on to explain.

'I have put adverts in magazines and on the internet to tell the world to come along and take part and to organise events in their own countries. Its all going to take place simultaneously the world over, millions of people will have an orgasm at the same time. I've informed scientific establishments to be prepared with their seismometers at the ready and it should be interesting to see what the reading on the Richter scale will be. It will give a whole new meaning to the expression "Did the earth move for you?" What do you think?'

'Gemma, I am speechless. If you can pull it off it will be amazing.'

Our conversation was cut short by the sound of applause from the dining room. We walked over to see what the excitement was.

It was David; he was showing off and demonstrating his sex aid. I had not seen it erect, if you pardon the pun, but basically it consisted of a bench that was made up of black padded vinyl boards of various sizes, supported by a black tubular steel framework that extended up and over the bench. From this hung various chains with leather strap manacles attached and a sort of sling that looked like a ships hammock. David went on to explain with great enthusiasm that every part of the device was adjustable in both height and width to accommodate a variety of sex acts. Explanation over, a series of practical demonstrations were required and Ted and Sheila, being the hosts were the first to try it.

Sheila stood at the side of the bench her nipples standing proud from her shirt. Ted stood before her and removed his clothes. Everyone was silent as Ted stood naked in front of his wife. It was fascinating to watch his penis transform from soft dangly flesh into a rod of iron. He stepped towards Sheila and seized her roughly in his arms and kissed her passionately. He stood back a little and took her shirt in his hands and ripped it open revealing her firm large round breasts that shook with the force. Ted pulled her shirt down her arms and tossed it aside; he then took the front of her knickers with both hands and with one swift snatch, ripped them from her. My pussy was twitching and becoming very wet at watching this primitive but exciting spectacle. Ted took her arm roughly and virtually dragged his naked wife to the foot of the bench and turned her to face it, there he grasped a manacle and strapped it to her wrist then pulling the chain tight which stretched her arm up to a corner of the framework. He then repeated the operation with her other arm, she cried with pain as he wrenched her arms. Then he secured her ankles to the bottom corners of the framework. She was trapped and at his mercy, arms and legs stretched apart.

'You've been a naughty girl haven't you my dear.' Said Ted in an evil voice.

'Yes.' Whimpered Sheila.

'And you know what happens to wicked girls don't you?' Sneered

Ted as he strutted up and down with his hands on his hips and his huge erection before him.

'Yes.' Whimpered Sheila again.

'I'm going to whip you.'

'No, please, not that.' Pleaded Sheila.

'Oh yes my dear; that.' He laughed mockingly and extended his right hand and on cue someone handed his a multi stranded whip. 'Six strokes.' He announced.

'Please have mercy.' Cried Sheila.

'Bad girls are shown no mercy.' He scowled. Then rose up the whip and with a look of evil on his face the whip whistled through he air and with a crack burnt into Sheila's bare flesh. She threw her head back and screamed.

'One.' Said Ted with a demeaning attitude. He lifted his arm high again and with equal determination and ferocity he let the whip fly. Once more the lash gouged into her flesh and once more she screamed. As the whip descended Ted had a look of decadent pleasure on his face and his penis, still rock hard quivered slightly with the force.

'Two.'

He raised his arm again and let the lash fly. It whistled through the air and slapped hard onto Sheila's back. She screamed out again with pain and seemed to just hang from her chains. A young woman at the back ran out crying.

'Three.'

Her back was now covered with red streaks and once more the lash rained down on her. Sheila didn't scream, she just let out a gargled grunt and arched her back.

'Four.' Announced Ted with his sadistic joy.

I was beginning to become concerned and wondered if things had gone too far. Another whistle and slap and Sheila screamed out once more and she cried. Tears rolled down her cheeks as her broken body hung from the chains that bound her.

'Five.'

The last lash crashed into her flesh again and it was almost as if Ted had summoned up all the effort of the last five and put it into this one. Her back and buttocks were bright red and raw. She let out an incredible scream and her back arched with the pain. She then slumped forward, her head just hanging loosely as she cried uncontrollably.

Then two women stepped forward and unshackled her. Sheila, still crying kneeled onto the bench. One of the young women took Ted's whip and gave him a small jar of cold cream and as if a changed person, benevolently and gently rubbed it into the lash marks. Sheila seemed to purr with pleasure as if magically the cream had taken away the pain. She was on all fours and she parted her legs wider and we could all see the wet pinkness of a very sex ready cunt. Ted took some of the cream and rubbed in on the length of his shaft. He stood behind her and eased it into her pouting vagina. Sheila screamed again, this time with pleasure as Ted rammed his mighty cock deeply inside her cunt. He grasped her hips with his hands and rammed her hard like an animal. He thrust his cock into her and pulled her hips onto him, his cock like a mighty dagger stabbing into her cunt.

'Harder.' She ordered. 'Fuck me harder.'

Ted pumped his cock into her hungry cunt as hard as he could. I could clearly see his shaft stretching her cunt as it went in the whole length and I could see his balls shaking and slapping against her.

'Harder you bastard,' She shouted with aggression and this was from the women who a few minutes earlier seemed to be dying from her ordeal. Now she was a demanding insatiable nymphomaniac.

Ted thrust valiantly but it seemed clear that he was about to ejaculate and his preying mantis of a wife wanted a lot more. His fingers dug into her hips as he let out a scream of pleasure and with a few more deep thrusts Ted came and shot his load into her. His cock squelched inside her as he filled her cunt with his hot semen. He gave a few more exhausted thrusts, but he was a spent force.

'I'm sorry my dear, it was so beautiful, I couldn't hold it. Please forgive me.' He whimpered like a lamb.

She turned to look back at him with a look of absolute venom on her face.

'You have failed me.' She said almost sounding like the growl of a tigress. 'And you know what happens to failures don't you?'

Ted was silent and frozen with fear.

'Don't you?' She snarled loudly.

'Yes.' Jumped Ted.

He stepped back his cock now descending and dripping with semen. Sheila got off the bench and walked around a whimpering Ted like the panther she had turned into. She snapped her fingers and the two young women stepped forward and shackled Ted to the frame work and as he hung there as helpless as she did earlier, she dispensed out his punishment. Six lashes. Ted screamed as she did and with every lash, the effort made her breasts bounce and clap together and I felt sure that Ted's was the only cock in the house that was soft.

After his lashing was over Sheila gave the order to cut him down. The two women unshackled him and lay him on the bench, face up, then re-shackled his ankles and shackled his outstretched arms. Two small panels were removed from the top of the bench so that just the centre part supported Ted's head. The height of the bench was lifted and Sheila's mighty thighs straddled his head. She lowered her vulva onto his mouth.

'Now lick your semen out of me you toad, and lick me until I come and if you fail me again it will be six more lashes.' Ordered Sheila as she leaned forward and gripped the bench either side of Ted's chest.

We could hear the lapping of Ted's tongue against her clitoris as he stimulated her and tasted his own come. Sheila started to moan with pleasure straight away; it was obvious that Ted was going to score this time. By now my knickers were soaked with love juice and it was obvious from the twitching from everyone else they wanted a piece of the action. But back to Ted and Sheila, she was obviously into it because her hips were sliding back and forth over Ted's mouth and as she leaned forward her tits swayed with the motion. Ted was gripping his chains and Sheila was rubbing her cunt into his mouth even harder. Her face was screwed up with the agony of pleasure and suddenly she let out a shriek of pleasure and her eyes were wide open and staring madly as the rush of immaculate pleasure took over her whole body. She gripped two uprights on the frame as she screamed out in pleasure and smothered Ted's mouth with her sucking fucking cunt.

By this time Ted was erect again and most of the audience were gasping for it. Gemma had lost her skirt and knickers and just stood there with her necklace on. It was all too much for her, she was fingering her clitoris but she wanted cock and she wanted it now. The bench was lowered and two outer boards were removed so Ted lay on only a thin board. Gemma mounted him and guided his cock into her cunt. With her feet on the floor and holding on to two uprights she rode him to ultimate pleasure. She had complete control with her feet on the ground and something to hold onto. She slid back and forth her mighty tits shaking up and down and slapping together. Within minutes she too screamed out with the ultimate pleasure as the ecstasy ripped through her body.

I was aching for it, literally in pain for want of sex. Eventually, the bench was vacant and I being the wife of the inventor was entitled to have the next go. David put back the two board sides as if he knew what he was to demonstrate next. I stripped naked and grabbed Roger; I was going to break him in. I lay on the bench with my legs open; not very subtle I know but let's face it that's what we are all here for. Roger quickly got undressed and when he took off his underpants a gasp went up from everyone. Everyone stared in stunned silence just looking at his ten inch cock, and I was going to have it.

David reached between my legs and took a six inch square panel out of the bench.
  'What's that?' I asked.
  'You'll see.' Was his reply, as he switched on the T.V.
  Then I saw it was a porno movie, and then I thought no, that's my pussy. He's got a camera under the bench. Then Roger's cock came into shot and I reached down and guided his purple cock head into me. It was incredible to watch this huge cock sliding into my tight little cunt. I could see it stretching my labial flesh as it slid into me, the rim of his bulbous end rubbing away at my inside. Not only see it, but feel it as well, it was an unbelievably erotic experience. After all that we had been watching I didn't need any foreplay, I was so excited I just wanted a good hard fuck and I was going to get it. It also gave it a new erotic dimension knowing that everyone was watching me being fucked in such close up intimate

detail. Roger was a demon and his cock filled my cunt and with every thrust I felt it stretch me. Watching the screen I could see that his whole length wouldn't go in but with every thrust he tried and it was beautiful. With every thrust I tried to suck him in further. Eventually I could feel pleasure waves radiating out from my cunt to my whole body. That unbelievable feeling of total wanton abandon that spiralled up and took over everything. It built up and up and I held my breath to hold it back so it would get higher and higher. It reached boiling point and I could hold it no longer, that rippling wave of unimaginable pleasure raced through my body and I screamed out at the top of my voice. On the screen Roger was thrusting harder and harder then he too screamed out in agony of pleasure and I felt his huge cock get bigger inside me and let forth a torrent of hot pulsating semen. His balls seemed to squeeze themselves as they shook about in his scrotum banging against my thighs. His semen shot inside me and filled me and then squelched out and on the screen his huge cock was dripping with it.

I lay there fucked and exhausted. It had been brilliant and I hoped Roger would become one of our regulars. We didn't lie there long as we were politely requested to vacate the bench as a queue was forming.

The evening turned into a weekend and David's Bondage bench was a great success and in constant use. I never saw the hammock thing being used however, but I'm told it was used and that part of it, along with the bench doubled up as a device that would sleep two people. Very handy, as so many people slept over.

SYLVIA AND DENNIS

We had just finished breakfast and I gathered up the dishes and placed them in the sink. I was still in my nightie and dressing gown but George was dressed and raring to go. At eight o'clock sharp the minibus pulled up outside and the driver gave a short toot on his horn. George was having a very deserving few days away with his old army pals. He had been invalided out some ten years ago due to a training exercise that went tragically wrong and a fall had left him wheelchair bound. Since then we had lived a steady life here in our beautiful home with manicured gardens, a barbeque patio and all the other trimmings of successful middle class suburbia. In an ideal world probably not the lifestyle of choice for George, but his situation dictated our future somewhat. He was obviously bitter about the cruel hand of fate he had been dealt, but being an officer and a gentleman, bit the bullet and kept a stiff upper lip. On the plus side he was awarded a very generous pension and now we were settled in one place I was able to pursue a very lucrative career in the broadcasting industry. So we had a comfortable if somewhat restricted lifestyle.

George refused to let his disability get him down and had thrown himself enthusiastically into whatever sport and pastime he could. He competed regularly and successfully in paraplegic marathons. Shooting and archery were two other sports he excelled in, but his greatest passion was for flying and he was a qualified micro-light pilot and this was what he was indulging in this weekend. I admired his spirit enormously and was grateful he still had that zest for life and passion for flight. I suppose it was ironic really, a man unable to walk, but was in a way a master of the sky and had the freedom of the birds. Lesser men in similar circumstances would probably have become bitter and introverted by their misfortune, but not George and I loved and respected him enormously for it. There was however one glaring omission in our lives and that was our sex life, I did miss that and so I assume did George, but he never complained, or even mentioned it. But apart from that, well…

The door bell rang, it was Bert the driver. I opened the door and he reached in for George's suitcase.

'Morning Sylvia.'

'Morning Bert, how are you?'

'Mighty fine, mighty fine. Is the miserable old bastard ready?'

'Less of the old.' Said George wheeling through from the lounge.

'How are you George?' He greeted.

'Never better old boy. Got those birds ready for the sky?'

'You bet Skipper. Fuelled up and ready to fly.' Beamed Bert.

George gave me a quick kiss goodbye and to a cheer from the passengers on the bus, free- wheeled down the drive, a sharp right turn at the bottom and slid effortlessly on to the tail lift of the minibus. To a welter of handshakes and excited conversations, George was now in another world. Bert secured the ramp and closed the back door and gave me a little wave. He got back in the cab and drove off. George gave a little wave after being nudged by one of his pals and they were gone. I didn't mind him not giving a long wave or blowing a kiss or anything like that. Anyway it was never George's way and he had the thoughts of soaring with the birds with the rest of the squadron foremost on his mind. I gave a sigh and closed the front door.

I walked into the lounge and the house seemed suddenly larger and silent. George was indeed a presence and now he was gone for the weekend I felt lost and slightly lonely. In strange way however I did enjoy these weekends of solitude, it gave me time to think and I had started to write a novel, a bit of nonsense really but it gave me a goal in life. "You must have goals in life." George always used to say. "Because without goals, life becomes meaningless." And I'm sure he was right. I looked at our wedding photo on the shelf and I felt my eyes filling with tears. George looked very dashing in his uniform and even now he still had a good physique, it was just a tragedy that it wasn't in a hundred percent working order. Still, what's done is done and nothing can be done about it. I'm just grateful that George is able to cope with it, in his own way.

I went upstairs to shower and dress. I pulled open the dressing table drawer to select suitable clothing for the day. A long loose skirt and a salmon colored thin top. It looked as though it would be a warm day so I wanted something loose and cool. I threw them onto the bed along with suitable underwear. Looking at myself in the mirror I could see that time and gravity were beginning to take their toll on my body and also my hair needed a little attention. But having said that for someone in their early fifties, I wasn't too bad. I had colored my hair a platinum blond, which was quite commonplace I know, but it looked natural and the grey roots that invariably came through didn't shout out as loudly as if it was darkly colored. It was also cut in a very safe and ordinary style, neck length all the way round, so it curled under, parted in the middle, with a full fringe. My face was nothing special, but I had a small nose that used to "wrinkle cutely" as George put it, whenever I smiled. He also said I had "interesting teeth", whatever that meant. But coming from George, whose compliments about any subject were rare, was an accolade indeed. I was quite short in stature, just a little over five feet and as with a lot of short people I tended to be broad and curvy and thick set. Not fat exactly, but of a fuller figure as the polite critic would say which meant a big backside and a big bust. When I stood and held my stomach in and stuck my chest out it was quite eye-catching, but as my cheeks were puffed out and my face was turning red, it was not a posture I could keep up for long. Turning side on, I had a bit of a paunch when I let it all go. I turned to face the mirror again and I let my hand slide down across my tummy until it flowed over my pubic mound and slide gently through my lips. I shuddered with pleasure as my middle finger lightly caressed my clitoris. There was an area that had been denied proper attention for a long time. I sighed thoughtfully and went for my shower.

Hanging the towel over the radiator I returned to the bedroom to dress. I pulled on my panties and stepped into my skirt and as I pulled it up to my waist I could still feel my pussy tingling with pleasure. My nipples were erect and I was in two minds as to whether to strip off and relieve myself of this sexual volcano that was building up inside me. Then the decision was made for me as there was a knock on the door. I reached for my bra and noticed the strap was broken. I knew it was on the verge and I meant to repair it and keep it for emergencies but obviously the rigours of the washing machine had finished it off. The door sounded again. I saw through the window that it was a delivery van, probably with George's wine, so rather than miss it and have to make other arrangements I just put on my top and raced down stairs before they disappeared. As I came down I could feel my breasts bouncing about and with my top being so loose and low cut, one of them bounced out, how I don't know, but I just pulled my top out and up and let it fall back in. With a deep breath and a cough I composed myself and opened the door.

The delivery man was about twenty in a smart company uniform and I must admit he looked quite appealing. His eyes immediately zeroed in on my nipples and as I glanced down they stuck out like plums. In embarrassment I immediately folded my arms.

'Er, delivery for you madam.' He said politely and coughed nervously. He then gave me an electronic note-book to sign, which I did awkwardly as I was trying to cover my nipples with my forearms.

'Shall I carry it in for you, it is rather heavy?' He said taking back his note book.

'Thank you, yes.' I replied, grateful for not having had to lift it and also so I didn't give a display of sagging breasts by bending down. 'Could you put it on the kitchen table for me?'

'Certainly.' He pocketed his electronic device and swept the box up effortlessly.

I automatically closed the front door and guided him through to the kitchen.

'Alright here?' he said as he lowered the box onto the table.

'That's absolutely fine. Thank you very much.'

'My pleasure Mrs. Redman.'

I was flattered and pleased at being treated with such respect, as most people these days just drop off your delivery and push a pad and pen at you without speaking then leave silently with equal lack of manners and usually pulling up their trousers over their buttock cleavage as they depart. As I gestured to show him out I had a flash of recognition about him but could not place his face. 'Thanks again, you've been most helpful.'

'All part of the service Mrs. Redman.' He replied with a smile. 'You don't remember me do you?' He continued.

'Well your face is familiar.' I said slowly and trying to get my brain into gear.

'I'm Dennis Wilson; I used to live at number thirty eight.'

'Of course, Deborah and Stephen's son.' I said relieved. 'My word that takes me back. How are your Mum and Dad?'

'They're fine. Both retired now.'

'And you, I suppose you're married now.'

'No afraid not.'

'Have you time for a coffee?' I asked. The words came out automatically and I felt it was something in my subconscious that compelled me to say it.

'Yes, I'd love one.'

I invited him to sit at the table and I prepared the coffee. Dennis had turned into a very attractive young man and I was ashamed at the thoughts that were going through my mind. As I filled the kettle I glanced down and could see that my nipples were still erect. Here I was with a man half my age and I was having lustful thoughts about him. In my mind I rebuked myself and told myself not to be a fool. A few minutes later we were sitting opposite each other sipping our hot coffee. I noticed Dennis eyeing my bust again, I didn't realise it but my bust was resting on the table and was spreading out like a jelly. I quickly sat upright and tried to adopt a more ladylike posture.

'Isn't Mr Redman at home today?' Asked Dennis.

'No, he is away at the flying club for the weekend.' I said. 'Would you like a biscuit Dennis?' I said, suddenly finding making conversation surprisingly difficult.

'Oh, no thank you Mrs. Redman.' He said with a hint of nervousness in his voice.

I leaned forward across the table and put my hand on his. 'Please, call me Sylvia.' And as soon as I said it I realised that I had opened a door that I may later regret opening.

'Oh, er, right, thank you... Sylvia.' He stammered. 'I have always had a great admiration of you.' He said slowly after taking a deep breath.

'Thank you Dennis, that is sweet of you.' I squeezed his hand again and he squeezed it back. I was very flattered at his comment and the obvious courage he had to summon up to say it. I wanted to make love to this young man and I wanted it desperately, whatever the consequences. I loved George dearly but I wanted a man's physical love, I wanted sex. I wanted sex with Dennis.

'Are you seeing anyone at the moment?' I said in a low and sultry voice, keeping his gaze at the same time.

He swallowed nervously. 'No.' He squeaked. 'No, not at the moment.' He said after clearing his throat. 'Actually, I have been delivering around here for some time and I have been trying to pluck up courage to call, I've even thought of calling by pretending I had the wrong address. So I was really pleased when I got a proper delivery. Sorry, I'm rambling.'

'That's alright, just relax.' I said taking his hand and squeezing it reassuringly. 'You should have just come, we would have been glad to see an old friend again.'

'I used to day dream about you Sylvia.'

'Well that's nice, really flattering.' I said, and the truth was that I was more than flattered, in fact my vagina was getting very wet. This shy naive young man intrigued me. 'And what sort of things did you dream about Dennis?' I continued in my sultry voice.

'You know... things.' He said nervously.

'Like... kissing me, kissing me passionately.

'Yes.'

'Did you imagine me naked, on the bed?'

'Yes.'

'And did you make love to me?'

'Yes.'

'And what did you do, when you were dreaming of making love to me?' I said, knowing full well what a boy of sixteen would be doing, but I wanted to hear him say it.

'I er...'

'Yes?'

'You know.' He stammered looking down at his coffee, his cheeks beginning to blush.

'Go on Dennis; tell me what you did when you were dreaming of making love to me.' I said teasing him terribly.

'I er, masturbated.' He said slowly. 'I suppose you're ashamed of me now aren't you?' He said guiltily.

'Not at all, there's nothing to be ashamed of, in fact I'm very flattered that I was the centre of your sexual fantasy.' I said reassuringly.

'Are you sure.' He said with enthusiasm and relief. I feel much better now I've opened up to you.'

My vagina was tingling incredibly at the thought of Dennis jerking himself off at the fantasy of my nakedness and I dearly wanted him to act out his fantasy for me.

I stood up and taking his hands I lifted him to his feet and away from the table. 'Kiss me Dennis.'

He took me in his arms and gave me the longest, most passionate kiss I have had in my life. 'Woo, that was some kiss.'

'Oh Sylvia.'

I took him upstairs to the bed room. He stood there looking nervous but excited, I went over to the bed and lifted my top over my head and threw it aside. Dennis gasped as he feasted his eyes on my breasts. I pushed down my skirt and panties together and let them fall to the floor. Casually kicking them aside I stood naked for Dennis to relive his adolescent fantasy.

'You look even better than in my dreams.' He sighed.

'It will be even better if you take your clothes off.' I said.

With that he started to undress. He was obviously very inexperienced, which I found all the more attractive, and he clumsily tried to unbutton his shirt with his trembling fingers. I stepped forward to help him and unbuttoned his shirt. I pulled it out of his trousers and pushed it from his shoulders, he looked wonderful and athletic. I let my hands cascade down his chest and over his muscular stomach, my fingers rippling and examining his every muscular contour. I reached his trouser belt and undid it, and then I let my hand slide down to feel his manhood through his trousers. It felt wonderfully firm and erect. Unclipping his trousers and slowly pulling down his zip, I felt his erect manhood shift position within his shorts. I pushed his trousers and they fell to the floor. I put my right arm around his shoulders, pulling him down to kiss me. He took my breast and fondled it lovingly; at the same time I slipped my other hand down the front of his shorts and found his huge cock. He sighed as I gripped it, rubbing my hand gently along its throbbing length. I slowly sank to my knees and peeled down his shorts and as I did so, his erect penis twanged to attention. He certainly was quite well endowed and I could tell he was eager but I had my own ideas. At the foot of the bed was a round back upholstered chair and behind it was a full length mirror. 'Sit down Dennis.' I instructed. He was puzzled but did as he was told. 'Now then, about your fantasies, can you imagine them now?'

'Oh yes, as if they were yesterday.'

'And you masturbated as you thought about having sex with me?'

'Yes.'

'Well I want you to masturbate for me now.'

'Alright.' He replied a little nervously.

I took a vibrator from my bedside drawer and lay on the bed with my feet towards Dennis. I had piled up the pillows so I was not quite in a sitting position, but not lying flat either. Dennis watched with fascination, gently stroking his shaft. I opened my legs and lifted my knees so he had a full view of my womanhood. 'Do you like the look of my pussy Dennis?'

'Oh God yes.'

'Is it like you imagined?'

'Better, much better.'

I slowly slid my hands down my belly and with the middle finger of each hand I pulled my vulva open.'

'Oh God.' Gasped Dennis and I could see my reflection in the mirror. This exhibition was a real turn on for me, the feeling of power I had over this young man was intoxicating and from my reflection I could see my love juice glistening on my lips. I reached for my vibrator and turned it on; I gave a little squeal of delight as the buzzing tip touched my clitoris.

It was a big one of ten inches in length. I smiled at Dennis as I gently manoeuvred the tip between my eager sucking lips. 'What do you think Dennis?' I asked.

'Fucking brilliant.' He gasped, his tone taking on an air of urgency.

I moaned loudly as I pushed the vibrator inside me. Slowly, inch by erotic inch it slid inside. It stretched me almost to a pain of great pleasure. I pushed it up as far as it would go. This huge plastic cock filled my cunt completely.

'Now it's your turn. I want to see you jerk yourself off; I want to hear you scream with pleasure. I want to see your semen shoot out of your cock.' He did as he was told and he rubbed his cock furiously with his right hand, moaning and muttering as he did so. His eyes never left the vibrator which I was now thrusting in and out of my cunt as fast as he was jerking himself off. It was new, it was thrilling, we were both masturbating and being thrilled by watching each other and I could see myself in the mirror performing this wanton act, my body shaking with the sheer energy of lust, my tits shaking in wild abandon. I thrust faster and faster and he thrust faster and faster. The vibrator was going in as far as I could take it and as it pulled out the vibrations teased my clitoris closer to orgasm.

'Oh God Sylvia I'm coming.' Cried out Dennis. Then his face contorted and his eyes rolled as jets of semen shot into the air. I was amazed and thrilled at the sheer amount he ejaculated. As he worked his shaft faster it continued to spurt out of him in huge pulses, squirting and shooting in all directions, followed by a lava flow of more semen cascading over his fingers. It was brilliant to watch this young man reaching ecstasy as he watched me fucking myself with a huge vibrator. It was enough to push me over the edge and I let out an almighty scream as I felt my orgasm building up to volcanic proportions and released ripples of pure pleasure through my body. My cunt tightened and sucked the vibrator further into me. Eventually it levelled off and died down. It was one of the most fulfilling orgasms that I have ever had. I watched in the mirror as I pulled it out and listening to my love juice squelching as I did so. Dennis lay slumped and breathing slowly in the chair, his mighty cock now deflating and still oozing semen and the initial ejaculation lay in strands on his belly and his fingers. A fantasy fulfilled.

FIRST AIDER

'Oh shit,' I said to myself, as I looked at my watch for the thousandth time this morning, it was Thursday and still only eleven o'clock. The end of the day seemed a long way off and the end of the week seemed an even longer way off. I was sitting at my desk typing an endless procession of letters and to say that the job was getting me down was something of an understatement. But there again I shouldn't really complain because I would be a lot worse off without it. The money was good but the prospects were not exciting and the job itself was not very fulfilling. Still it paid the bills and at the end of the day that is what mattered.

I looked out of the window and sighed. Another lorry entered the yard, Bernard came out of his little hut and checked the details on his clipboard and gave the driver directions to one of eight loading bays, whichever pertained most to his particular delivery. Bernard was two years off retirement and had been doing that job for the last twenty five years, he was happy and he loved his job. I suppose it gave him a real sense of purpose in life, directing drivers to a loading bay. In some ways I envied his outlook on life, but then again I felt sorry for him, after all he had only two years to go and then retirement. I could not help but think of my grandfather, he had a similar simple job that entailed the minor authority of a gate keeper. It was in his power to let someone in, or not. Never had a day off in forty years and worked from six in the morning till six at night six days a week. Sunday was spent in the garden or greenhouse whatever the weather or time of year, only seeing grandma at mealtimes and bedtime. His life fell apart when he retired, as his purpose in life was taken from him, and after six months of inane daytime television, he was gone. Was that a fate that awaited Bernard? Indeed was that a fate that awaited me? I gave a little shiver and continued with my typing.

'Morning Angela.' Said Mavis, the office manager. She breezed in, dropped a handful of papers for processing and filing in my in-tray, picked up my letters from the out-tray and took them away for signing and posting, without another word. Mavis was always in a hurry. She was another example of a live to work automaton, not very cheerful, not very young and not very married. I don't think she was gay or anything, but she just didn't seem to be able to hold down a steady relationship. Its not that she was bad looking, its just she seemed very uptight. She needed to de-stress and learn to open her legs a bit more. I gave another sigh and looked at my watch, it was five past eleven, and a whole five minutes had passed. I pondered a visit to the ladies room, but I only went twenty minutes ago, and I didn't really want to go then. Every tuk, tuk, tuk of the keyboard seemed to grate against my brain.

The office door opened again and it was Mavis.
'Angela dear, you are still the first aider aren't you?'
'Yes.' I said glad of the break from the monotony.
'Good show, I've got a casualty for you. Barry from design and development has stabbed himself with his scalpel.'
'Hello.' Said a pale faced Barry looking around the door frame.
'Don't go in dear,' said an unsympathetic Mavis, 'we don't want blood on the new carpet do we.'
'Oh right.' He said.
'Take him down to the medical room will you and do whatever is necessary.' Continued Mavis, then disappeared to attend to more important matters.
I went into the corridor to asses the casualty's situation. 'I know it's not the best place in the world to work, but isn't stabbing yourself with a scalpel taking things a little too far?'

'Well I didn't intend doing it, its just the scalpel was sliding and I had my hands full and I tried to stop it falling off the desk with my thigh and it turned and stuck in me.'

Barry was holding a paper tissue against the wound. It was bleeding, but not seriously and he was walking, so hopefully hospitalisation would not be necessary.

'Come on then, I'll take you to the medical room and see what's what.' This was a very welcome break from the routine and I was going to play it for as long as possible.

'I saw you in the social club last week.' Said Barry.

'Oh yes.'

'Yes.'

I had to admit that Barry wasn't bad looking but the originality of his chat up line was close to zero.

'Shall you be going there again?' He continued.

'I expect so.' I replied.

'Good, I'll probably see you there then.'

I couldn't help thinking that this was an invite to a date but the words came out in the wrong order and with some of them missing. Still I would be in his company for the immediate future so he had time to re-evaluate the situation and try again.

'This is it.' I said as we approached the medical room.

'Oh yes, medical room, it says so on the door. Sorry, loss of blood making me ramble, sorry'.

I smiled at him; his nervous naivety was very amusing, and as we were talking in the corridor I thought I heard noises in the medical room and wondered if there was another casualty already in there. I knocked. No answer, so I slowly opened the door and peered in. It was empty so I entered. 'Come on Barry lets get your thigh sorted.

The medical room was a bit basic; it had a bench like couch, the sort of thing you see in a doctors surgery, a sink, medical cabinet and a store room which usually contained cleaning equipment and toilet rolls etc. 'Sit down Barry.' I said indicating the bed. I also realised that because of the nature of his injury he would have to take his trousers off. Things were beginning to look up I thought.

'Er, do I need to take my trousers off?' He said, almost reading my mind.

'Well I could cut them off, just above the wound but you're going to look a bit silly when you get back to work.'

'With one trouser leg shorter than the other you mean?'

I had to admit that Barry was not the sharpest of characters and I indeed wondered how he even managed to put his trousers on in the first place, anyway what he lacked in wit, he more than made up for in looks.

'Right, let's have the trousers off then.' I commanded.

Barry took off his slightly blood stained trousers and folded them neatly and draped them over a chair. He looked very attractive standing in his t-shirt and boxer shorts. He had athletic muscular shoulders, trim waist and well developed muscular thighs and his shorts gave the outline of promising delights within. His thigh was bleeding, but it wasn't much and a wipe with a sterile swab and a plaster would do the trick. So I got the necessary equipment out of the medical cabinet, cotton wool, alcohol and suitable sized plaster.

'Lie on the couch and lets take a look at it.' He did as he was told and I couldn't help thinking that I had him at my advantage. I pulled off a swab of cotton wool from the roll and soaked it in alcohol and dabbed it on his wound. Barry winced slightly.

'It stings.' He whispered.

'Well we don't want an infection do we?' I said as I continued to wipe the area in ever widening circles. The wound was at the top of his thigh so I pulled up the leg of his shorts slightly and I felt my two fingers touch the end of his penis. He winced again.

'Sorry.' I said.

'No, it was nice.'

A boring day was now getting very interesting I thought and I pulled back the leg of his shorts again so his penis was now visible and growing at an alarming rate. I stroked it gently as he lay there gently moaning with pleasure and he moaned louder as I pulled back his shorts even further to reveal his swelling glans. Time was of the essence and I was feeling really randy and here was a chance of doing something worth writing in my diary. So putting the day job to the back of my mind and concentrating on the welfare of my patient, I undid and removed my blouse, dropped my skirt to the floor, unclipped and threw off my bra and whipped off my knickers. I was completely naked, beautiful, free and naked.

Barry sat up on his elbows, his mouth wide open in amazement and his shaft was fully erect and sticking awkwardly from the leg of his shorts and it was indeed a beauty.

'Well.' I said letting my hands follow the contours of my body. He didn't need another prompt and at last showed some initiative. He swivelled off the couch and dropped his shorts, and his huge shaft waved at me. Then almost as an afterthought he peeled off his t-shirt revealing his very lean and taught body. I quickly lowered the height of the couch to what I thought would be a good level for what I was thinking of might develop later. Barry came towards me and gathered me up in his strong arms and kissed me. He surprised me pleasantly, because what I thought was a stumbling piece of beefcake was now showing himself as a very experienced and competent lover. He kissed me passionately and longingly and as he held me I could feel his erect shaft sticking into my belly. I followed my instincts and let my hand slide down his side to his hips. He knew where I was going so lessened his grip on me so I could slide my hand across until I found his shaft and what a shaft it was, my fingers only just reached around its thickness. I let my hand slide up and down it, following every contour and every vein; I felt his big bulbous glans with its proud ridge, imagining it rubbing the sides of my vagina and bringing me to a climax. I could clearly feel it pulsate and throb, it was like a caged animal that wanted its freedom. I would give it its freedom, in time. I continued to let my hand caress its magnificence, up and down, not too fast just enough to keep him excited. Barry continued to kiss me and as he did so he continued to moan with pleasure. I pulled away from him, a strand of saliva breaking between us. We looked silently into each others eyes. Both of us knew the inevitable. I kissed his chest and slowly, ever so slowly I kissed lower and lower. I slowly kneeled down, his huge shaft still in my hand. A pearl like bead of semen seeped from his penis, I gently licked it off, and its savoury saltines aroused me greatly. I kissed his cock end gently and each time I opened my mouth a little, until I knew Barry was really suffering with desire and I gently let my lips slide over it until his glans was in my mouth. I gently sucked and slavered over it, I felt Barry's hands at the back of my head. I knew what he wanted, he wanted me to take more of him but I made him wait. Gently and teasingly I sucked his huge purple end, I could feel it throbbing and expanding in my mouth. I continued to torment him and as I heard him moaning in desperation I let my lips slide down his shaft and felt his cock end at the back of my throat. Barry yelped with pleasure as I sucked him. My mouth slid up and down his cock like a virgin's cunt, taking him to the heights of pleasure. He gasped and groaned with delight.

'Enough for now.' He said pulling his shaft from my mouth. 'It's your turn for pleasure.'

He bent towards me and lifted me to my feet. He kissed me again and I felt his tongue thrusting down my throat like a rampant shaft. He sat on the couch and indicated me to sit on his right. I did so and he took me in his arms and kissed me most passionately again. His hand slid gently from my waist until it gently caressed my breast. His kissing became more tempestuous and he fondled me more roughly. He kissed my throat and gently down my chest until his hand pushed my breast up to meet his kiss. He kissed and sucked me and his hand travelled slowly down my stomach. I parted my legs in anticipation, my pussy was wet and ready and I could feel my lips parting and felt my love juice running, I wanted Barry. After a tantalisingly long journey his fingers gently stroked my wet pussy. His middle finger parted my wet lips further and found my clitoris. I squealed with delight as he stroked it gently, sending vibrations of pleasure throughout my body. He was so skilful and as he gently played with me I just melted and I knew I could not take much more of that beautiful finger fucking without me coming. All the time he was still sucking and biting my breast. He then slid further down and I felt his fingers part my quim and with a wet squelch two of them slid inside me. He gently pushed them in and out simulating intercourse. Then I could feel all his fingers tightly together were gently pushing in and out of me. After a few gentle thrusts he began to push a little harder and I felt myself being stretched as they went a little further in. On and on he went and

I could feel his knuckles pushing against me, trying to get inside. It was becoming slightly painful and yet it was exciting, I was being stretched and stretched. I lay back on the couch until my shoulders touched the wall. Barry, with his fingers still inside me kneeled on the floor between my thighs. I lifted my legs and put them over his shoulders and folded them behind his neck. He pushed again and I felt myself stretching, it was a beautiful agonising pain. He pushed again and I screamed out as his fist finally went inside me. It felt better now it was inside. No one had done this before and it felt brilliant, his fist filled my cunt and I was sent to new levels of pleasure as his hand thrust inside me like the biggest cock imaginable. On and on he thrust, his arm inside me as far as it would go. I felt him gently punching the top of my cunt.

Barry had another trick; he licked my clit as he fisted me. It was unbelievable, within seconds I knew I was coming and I would have the orgasm of a lifetime. He licked my clit faster and faster and thrust his fist inside me harder and harder. It was too much, I couldn't hold it, and I felt the shudder of orgasm pulsating through me. I screamed as I exploded. He licked and thrust faster and faster. It seemed the orgasm just kept going up and up, the pleasure was so intense I felt I was never going to come out of it. I felt my cunt sucking in Barry's arm, it was an incredibly tight fit and it seemed to want more. Eventually to my relief, it peaked and I began to level off. Barry gently eased his arm out of me and continued to lick and suck my clitty until I came down. That was the most wonderful fuck of all time.

I sat there gasping as Barry's unsatisfied erect cock, gently bobbed to the rhythm of his pulse.

'Finish me off please.' He begged.

I took him deeply into my mouth and clutching his hips I sucked him off, taking his cock in as deeply as I could. It didn't take long, Barry was almost there. He took my head in his hands and took over. He thrust his cock into my mouth almost choking me. Pulling my head back and forth at a terrific rate. I was becoming dizzy with the speed he was thrusting me. Then he moaned and I felt his cock swell up and with a final thrust of my head onto his cock he came and filled my mouth with pulsating jets of hot semen. I took it all and as he came down I sucked him dry. It was brilliant, my cunt was as sore as hell, but it was brilliant.

Suddenly I heard a noise from the store cupboard. We looked at each other in silence, there's someone in there I thought. Then I remembered the noise just before we entered, someone was here after all and they had been watching us. Barry, his huge cock now deflated and swinging as he walked, opened the store cupboard door. Inside were two very red faced and very naked personnel from packaging. Obviously in here for sex and we interrupted them. The man was erect and unsatisfied as was probably his girlfriend.

'Sorry.' He said. 'You caught us out and we nipped inside the cupboard to hide.'

'Yes, but we were most impressed with your performance.' Continued his girlfriend.

'Well let's see how you perform.' I said

'OK.' She said much to my surprise, or maybe not, perhaps our performance turned them on as much as it did for us.

Anyway, like a gazelle she jumped onto the couch and knelt on all fours at the end. Her boyfriend stood behind her and took her from behind. He held her hips and thrust his shaft up her cunt and gave it to her good and hard. She reached back and stimulated her clitoris with her finger. It was quite erotic to watch another couple shamelessly fucking for you and they were quite good. The entire magnificence of his shaft sank deeply into her tight little cunt and she squealed and whimpered with ecstasy. As he rammed her, she continued to finger herself into a frenzy and as his thrusts became more rapid, her hanging tits swayed back and forth. They both screamed in orgasm together and his cock squelched as he filled her cunt with his semen.

What a performance, we met up with Tina and John, as we discovered they were called, at the social club later in the week. As time went by my relationship with Barry grew closer and we even had the occasional foursome with Tina and John. Not a bad day after all as it turned out.

MUSIC OF LOVE

❀

The air felt fresh and beautiful and as I lay naked on the bed, I felt its clean, crisp tingle flow over me. It was one of those positive, good to be alive days and I decided to have a quick refreshing shower to start off the day. It certainly did the trick and as I towelled myself dry in the bedroom I could feel the gentle rush of the breeze over my naked breasts and hear the lapping of the curtains at the window, the edge of it gently brushing against my thigh as it flowed and waved in the wind. I scolded myself for walking about naked with the curtains open, you never know who might be looking, and then again I thought, well, in this place it is unlikely that anyone would be looking.

I felt my way back to the bathroom and hung up the towel. It was going to be a gorgeous day I told myself as I returned to the bedroom and I selected my clothes accordingly. I reached into my underwear drawer and pulled out a pair of panties and bra and placed them on the bed. In the wardrobe I fingered along the rail and selected a short sleeved cotton dress, removed it from its hanger and laid it on the bed with my underwear. I clumsily knocked my hair brush onto the floor as I reached for it, 'If only they would stay where they fell.' I said to myself as I groped around on all fours trying to feel for it. 'Got it.' I said in triumph, as I found it just under the bed. Struggling to my feet I gave my hair a quick brush through and ran my hand over it to check nothing was sticking out. I didn't go in for modern styles, there was just no point, I just wanted something that just required a brush through every morning; as long as it looked reasonable to the outside world I was happy.

After breakfast I went to the common room to relax and listen to a talking book. As I entered I could tell there weren't many in yet. I heard the scratchy whistle from someone's earphones, 'Morning.' I said.

'Morning Carol.' Came back the loud reply.

It was Yvonne, obviously deep into some heavy metal band. I sat myself down and decided to devote the morning to Agatha Christie. While fumbling with the wires someone sat heavily in the seat beside me.

'Ah Carol, I thought I heard you come in, there's a little favor I wish to ask you.'

I sighed as I realised my plans were thwarted. It was Donald the Centre's resident warden. 'Yes Donald, how can I help you?'

'We've a new chap coming in today and as you are our most senior inmate, I thought you might take him under your wing, so to speak, and show him the ropes as it were.'

I could tell by the tone of his voice that there was something else. 'Senior inmate!' I replied with an air of protest, 'I am thirty two; you make me sound like an old lag doing a ten stretch in a high security prison.'

'Sorry. No, you see, Michael is a bit of a difficult case.'

'And you want to palm him off on me.'

'Well it's not really like that Carol. You see, Michael was a keyboard player in a high profile rock group and a car crash has left him blind and he refuses to come to terms with it and I thought...'

'We are all blind Donald, that is why we are here and that is why you are here. Correct me if I'm wrong, but doesn't rehabilitation come under your job description?'

'Yes but you have a better gift of communication than I have and I think Michael would respond better to the more mature female guidance, and I would be eternally grateful if you could help me.'

'OK.' I sighed. 'When is he due?'

'Well actually he's here now; his brother is bringing him over.'

I heard footsteps shuffling on the carpet towards us.

'Michael, I would like to introduce you to Carol.' Said Donald.

'Hello Michael.' I said warmly.

'Er Carol is offering her hand Michael.' Continued Donald, nervously.

'I don't want her hand, I want my sight back.'

'Well I'll get off then.' Said Michael's brother apologetically.

'Yes you get off and get on with your life, while I rot in this shit hole.'

I lowered my hand, it seemed that this selfish bastard was going to take some dealing with and I could have strangled Donald for dumping him on me.

'Sit down with Carol, Michael and I'll bring over some coffee.'

'Don't touch me you creep.' Snapped Michael.

I heard him stumble against the armchair and fall to the ground.

'Let me help you.' I said.

'I can manage.'

'The chair is just behind you Michael.' Gasped Donald, as Michael grunted and floped into the chair.

'Are you alright?' I asked sympathetically.

'Of course I'm alright. I'm blind, what could be better?'

'I'll er, get that coffee.'

And Donald left us. There was silence. 'Well?'

'Well what?' He replied sharply.

'Are you going to tell me about yourself?'

'I had a car crash. I'm blind. My life's over. End of story.'

'Your life's not over Michael, there's…'

'Oh fuck off. I've heard it all before. The patronising, telling me I will come to terms with the situation. Well I fucking will not come to terms with it and no amount of talking from you bastards is going to change that. I don't want your pity or your help.'

I was incandescent with rage at his selfish attitude and I was adamant that I was having nothing more to do with him.

'Right,' I said as I stood up, 'I'll leave you to wallow in your own self pity, you arrogant bastard.'

'No.' He gasped in fear. Don't leave me.'

I felt his hand touch my forearm and as it slid down to find my hand, it was trembling with emotion. He held both my hands tightly, like a drowning man gripping onto a piece of driftwood. His hands were shaking and I could hear him breathing heavily.

'Don't leave me.' He repeated in a quiet and desperate voice. 'Don't leave me.'

From an aggressive defiant monster he seemed to change into a frightened little lamb. He sat there gripping my hands, his mind full of conflict and darkness. I felt suddenly different towards him and felt a little guilty about how brusquely I had spoken. Sitting before me now was a sad, fearful and vulnerable little boy. And as he continued to grip my hands in desperation I felt my eyes filling up and a single tear ran down my cheek. I whispered to him. 'Don't worry Michael, I shan't leave you.' He started to cry gently. I sat down again and pulling free one of my hands I reached into my bag for my tissues. I placed one in Michael's hand and he dried his eyes. Both hands now free I reached for another tissue and dried my own eyes. An air of constructive tranquillity descended as Donald arrived back with the coffee.

'I see you are both hitting it off nicely.' Said Donald with an air of relief. 'Cream and sugar?'

'Black, one sugar...please.' Replied Michael timidly.

Donald placed the mugs of coffee within reach and made a tactical withdrawal. There was silence for a few minutes, the only sound was from the sipping of the coffee and somewhere in the distance Yvonne's earphones still hissed and crackled.

'I'm very sorry Carol.'

'That's alright; you have every right to be angry, its part of the healing process.'

'Thank you for understanding and staying with me.'

'Donald tells me you play in a rock band.'

'Used to, I used to be a key board player, but what good is a blind man in a rock group.'

'Some of the most successful musicians in the world were blind; look at Stevie Wonder and Ray Charles for instance.'

'Yeah, well they're different.'

'Not at all. You could do it.'

'No, my confidence has gone. I haven't played since the accident; in fact I haven't done anything since the accident. Bella has gone.'

'Bella?'

'My girlfriend. As I say I haven't done anything since the accident.'

'Will you play for me?'

'I can't.'

'Yes you can. Please.'

'I don't know.'

I took his hand and lifted Michael to his feet. I led him gingerly to the piano, steering him carefully around the obstacles. I placed his hand on the piano and I heard him positioning the stool. The lid quietly lifted open and Michael felt his position on the keyboard. 'Play something romantic for me.'

Michael played Debussy's Claire De Lune, one of the most beautiful and haunting pieces of music in the world. As he played my eyes filled with tears again. The piece was beautiful and it was played by a master. When he had finished Michael once again dissolved into tears.

'I'm sorry,' he said, composing himself, 'it was my mother's favourite piece, she wanted me to be a classical pianist you know. It was played at her funeral; it always affects me like this.'

Over the next few weeks Michael's confidence grew and on many evenings the common room was filled with his beautiful music. As time went by his attitude slowly changed and he began to enjoy life, as he now had purpose. And I have to admit that this man who I hated almost as soon as I had met him now had a place in my heart and I was growing very fond of him. In fact I was growing more than fond of him; I was beginning to fall in love.

A few weeks later I came into the common room and heard a group of unfamiliar voices, they seemed in good spirits and I heard Michaels voice amongst them. I made my way towards them. 'Good morning.' I called.

'Carol, Carol, come here, great news.' Said Michael enthusiastically. 'Come and meet the lads, this is Doug and Tim.'

'Nice to meet you Carol, I'm Doug.' Said a voice that took my forearm and shook my hand vigorously. 'Mike has been telling me all about you and how you got him playing again.'

'Well, I didn't really do anything.' I said sort of apologetically.

'You made him live for his music again.' Said the other voice, taking my hand and shaking it with equal vigour. 'Keep up the good work and make sure he doesn't change his mind.'

'Well lets get things organised Doug.' Said Tim. 'Nice meeting you Carol.'

'You to er...'

'Tim.'

'Nice meeting you Tim.' The two of them left. 'Well what's this great news?'

'The band is recording a new album and they want me to play on it.' He said laughing with joy.

'That's fantastic news. I knew they wouldn't forget you.' I was really pleased for him and we embraced each other warmly.

As he held me there was silence, but it was a silence that was talking within us. I was in Michael's strong arms and his hand caressed my back. Feelings were stirring inside me and I could feel a kind of electricity coming from Michael. I was sure he could feel similar chemistry coming from me. The room felt empty, if there was any activity my mind had blanked it out. All I could hear and feel was Michael and I wanted him and the time was now. I stroked the back of his head and my fingers ran through his long thick wavy hair. His fingers gently touched my face; he stroked my cheek and held my chin pulling down gently opening my mouth. I felt his warm sweet breath on my face as his lips found mine and we kissed. We kissed long and passionately. Was anyone watching I thought, but really I didn't care. This was our moment. 'Come to bed.' I whispered. I took his hand and we silently walked to my room.

The curtains gently hissed as they blew in the breeze. I pulled them together. Michael took me in his arms once more and we kissed, we kissed with such passion, such love, such wanting. My whole body was tingling with new found feelings that needed satisfying. I was becoming very moist within and I wanted Michael to make love to me. We continued to kiss and once again I was running my fingers through his wonderful lion's mane. His hand slid up my side slowly and teasingly and I gasped with wanton pleasure as it found my breast and fondled it lovingly. Michael was breathing heavily and his hand reached behind my back and slowly unzipped my dress. I stepped back and pulled it forward from my shoulders and I let it fall to the floor. I could hear Michael pull off his shirt and felt a gentle draft as he tossed it aside. The sound of his zip and the gentle rush of his jeans, the clump of his shoes. Silence for a second, then I felt his powerful hands on my shoulders gently pulling me towards him. I felt his huge stiff penis gently prod my tummy as he hugged me; my hands ran down his muscular naked back and gently stroked his firm buttocks. I clutched each of them and as I did so he tensed them. I gripped them harder, pulling them apart and pulling his huge shaft further up my tummy. I wanted it inside me; I wanted it desperately, more than anything else in the world. As I pulled and squeezed his buttocks he thrust his hips up and down rubbing his shaft against my belly. He became more and more passionate and swiftly unclipped my bra sending it flying across the room and gliding his fingers down my side and into my panties, they slid down my thighs and onto the floor. I stepped out of them and we were naked. Michael kneeled down and took my breasts in his hands and kissed and sucked each nipple in turn. My head was swimming with carnal pleasure and I wanted to be fulfilled.

'Oh Michael, I love you.' I whispered. He stopped and stood up and held me close.

'I love you too Carol.'

We stood silently, holding each other, my mind and body wanted him. I was desperate to feel physical love, to feel his manhood inside me. I took a deep breath. 'Michael...' I whispered. 'I am a virgin.'

He did not speak and I was concerned that his feelings for me had cooled. I need not have worried, his left arm slid behind my legs, the other supported my back and he carried me to the bed and gently lay me down. He gently kissed my lips and slowly began to kiss my throat, my chest and clutching my breasts he sucked and kissed them passionately. He went lower and lower down my body and I opened my legs for him. He moved down the bed to lie between my thighs and kissed my knee, slowly going higher and higher. I was beginning to feel eager for his attention. Higher and higher he went and I felt his lips gently kiss my pussy lips. I felt very wet and excited and I wanted him inside me, I wanted him to take my virginity. He kissed me again and I could feel my vagina tingling and waiting to receive his manhood. Michael continued to tease me, his tongue gently following the contours of my womanhood. I gasped as I felt his tongue part my lips and gently run between them until it reached my clitoris. I moaned loudly as it made contact, it was an incredible feeling of indescribable pleasure. He continued to lick me and I was consumed with delight. I opened my legs wider, bent my knees and gripped my thighs so I could pull them open wider and higher giving Michael full vent and greater pleasure. Michael moaned with lust as he licked me faster and more vigorously. This was all new to me and the feeling was incredible, I had never experienced anything like it before. Before long the pleasure had reached an uncontrollable level, it seemed to be getting higher and higher. It was all consuming and a little frightening. My whole body seemed to be shaking as a feeling of earth shattering ecstasy washed over me. Michael sensed my feelings and licked me faster and faster. I wanted him to go on and on, this feeling was incredible, I was scared but I wanted to see where it would go. I felt it reaching a crescendo and I stopped breathing as my orgasm reached its peak and I screamed out loudly with pleasure. It seemed to roll around inside my body for an eternity. I felt out of control and powerless as this incredible feeling gripped and shook my body with pleasure. Michael continued to lick me as it went on and on, his licking seemingly to fuel the feeling. Eventually it seemed to level off and I gasped with delight. As I was in this limbo stage, still holding the backs of my thighs, Michael kneeled between my legs and gripped my hips lifting my bottom off the bed and supported me on his knees. I then felt the moment of truth was coming as I felt the head of Michael's shaft touch my vulva. Gently, ever so gently it began to part my lips and slide inside my vagina. It felt new and wonderful. Then I felt a slight pain, a burning sensation. Michael gently slid further inside me and I let out a little cry of pain as my maidenhead had been breached. He pushed his shaft further in to its full length and it was wonderful, my virginity was gone. Michael thrust his shaft inside me like a demon, stabbing me harder and harder. He quickly became overcome by passion and with a cry of pleasure; I felt his liquid ecstasy flood inside me. I had given myself to Michael completely and my virginity was no more.

The following week Michael was in a sombre mood, something was troubling him and he wouldn't tell me what it was. Eventually after dinner we walked in the garden, it was a beautiful evening but I could feel an atmosphere of foreboding. Eventually sitting down on a rustic bench, the scent of the garden on the breeze, he told me what was wrong. The group had signed up for a nationwide tour to promote the new album and that he was going with them. I felt devastated that my lover was going away but knew in my heart that I could not hold him back. My heart sank deeper when he said that Bella had come back into his life. I was devastated, I had to get away. I ran back to my room, grazing my legs on the furniture as I went. Tears filled my eyes and I could not help myself, I sobbed uncontrollably as I ran. I lay on my bed and cried and cried and cried. The days were endless and the nights were even longer. I could not come to terms with the fact that the only man I had ever loved was gone.

Days became weeks and weeks became months. I was nothing but an emotional wreck and I had a big problem. I sat in the common room late at night and a tear ran down my cheek. Silence and darkness. I began to doze in the chair and in that halfway state I dreamt of that haunting music of that eventful afternoon. I opened my eyes and I could still hear it. I felt disorientated, but gradually realised that this was no dream, someone was playing Debussy, that tune, our tune. I stood up and walked towards the piano.
    'Hello Carol.'
    'Michael.' I gasped. 'I thought you were on tour.'
    'I am on tour. We're on at the Lyceum tomorrow night.'
    'The Lyceum in town?'
    'That's the one. Would you like to come?'
    'What about Bella?'
    'We mutually decided to split.'
    'Oh I'm sorry.'
    'Don't be. I split because I want to be with you. I want to be with you, forever.'

'Oh God.' I said, once again the tears welling up.

'When I said I loved you I meant it. I want you to be my life partner. Will you do it?'

'Yes, God damn it, yes'.

'Good'. He said continuing to play.

'There's something else.'

'What's that?'

'I'm having your child.'

'That's nice. We'll have someone to mow the lawn then in a few years.' He said in a nonchalant matter of fact manner.

He stood up and we embraced. We were together forever, forever, in love.

THE MOVIE

Carl had been nurturing the idea of making *the* porno film to end all porno films for some time now and had pages and pages of script ideas, if a script for a porno film isn't too much of a paradox that is. Now after years of theorising and planning the project was finally coming together and filming was about to start. The idea of the film was to have as many people having sex at the same time as possible, in other words an all out orgy and Carl would be circulating with his cameras filming couples and groups in action. The cast was huge and a rota was devised so that various groups would slip into the arena as it were, at certain times so there would always be a fresh collection of bodies performing at any given moment, rather than having them all starting at once and all finishing at the same time. With this in mind Carl would be mingling within the writhing throng and filming his close ups and camera angles for many hours and hoping, after editing, for some classic porno footage.

The film was operating on a tight budget, in fact the performers, many of which were our friends from various swinging societies, plus friends of friends weren't being paid in cash. In fact they were basically doing it for the pleasure and the chance of getting their faces and more interesting bits in the movie. All they were offered were, unlimited quantities of beer and wine and all the buffet and barbeque food they could eat. There was a vague hint that the movie could possibly be introduced into the mainstream porno circuit, but personally I think that this was probably a long shot. But having said that, they were all promised a copy of the movie on DVD to keep so they could relive the joys of sex for many years to come, or cringe at their spreading waist lines or various other body parts that had succumbed to a combination of advancing years and the drooping effects of good living.

Carl had worked his brain to a standstill in formulating an invigorating plot and the storyline, as is the case in most films of this nature is very simple and undemanding on the mental faculties. Basically the storyline goes as follows, Carl and Gina, which is Carl and me, have organised a swingers weekend at our house. The party is just getting into the swing of things when Gina (me) answers the door bell and is presented with an incredibly handsome man asking for directions, as he has taken a wrong turning and is lost. As fate and the script would have it, this handsome chap is taking a bus load of other swingers to a swinger's party at a hotel that he can't find. As it happens the hotel in question is just around the block, but our heroine (me) feigns ignorance of its location and instead invites the handsome man and his coach load of swingers to join our bash. After a quick consultation they all agree and we have the makings of an epic movie. So in a nutshell that is a brief outline of Carl's cinematic masterpiece.

The first of our guests were soon to arrive and they would be in the first wave of the movie and as they were replaced by subsequent arrivals, they would be seconded into taking care of refreshments etc. after getting cleaned up of course, and maybe later in the evening if they got steam up again they could relieve the later stragglers and join in the finale.

I must admit that Carl had put a lot of thought into the technical side of this project. Not only had he got the latest camera and digital editing and copying equipment, but he had also set up a number of monitor screens throughout the house. These screens by means of some radio connection that I don't pretend to understand, were linked to Carl's camera, so in effect whatever he was filming would be displayed on all the screens. I can vouch for the fact that being able to watch yourself being fucked is a wonderfully erotic stimulant, as all mirror fuckers will gladly testify.

So the scene was set and the camera was ready. We were fortunate in that we had a large house with large rooms and the lounge was sparsely furnished for the evening with bean bags and scatter cushions and the like. The bedrooms had also been de-cluttered to give free access to the roving camera. Carl was twitching with excitement and for the last half hour had a permanent erection protruding menacingly inside his trousers. I dressed simply, and in keeping with the occasion, I wore a loose fitting white vest with no bra, so my tits rubbed against the material keeping my nipples constantly erect. I didn't wear a skirt, just cream colored French knickers so the lacy trims around my thighs showed teasingly below the level of the vest. I also wore self support stockings, that gave the same erotic effect to men without the need for suspenders and personally I think they looked better anyway. I don't know what it was about this combination that inflamed men so passionately, perhaps it was that glimpse of bare thigh flesh between stocking top and pantie leg, the promise of things to come perhaps. Anyway it never failed to get them going and I must admit I could feel a fluttering in my pussy at the thought of the power and of the night's forthcoming events.

The door bell sounded.

'They're here.' Shouted Carl excitedly.

I opened the door and it was Chelsea and Mike, two of our oldest friends and ardent swingers. They were both in their early forties and both were incredibly attractive. Chelsea had blond hair and blue eyes with a cute little nose, she also had a very pale complexion which was almost virgin like. She was wearing a pale three quarter coat with a simulated fur collar. Mike took the coat from her and we could all see the rest of her attributes, as she was completely naked underneath.

'Wow.' Gasped Carl.

'Saves time darling.' Responded Chelsea obviously raring to go.

Chelsea had a lovely figure with broad hips that many a man has enjoyed getting to grips with while fucking her from behind and incredible tits, that despite their large size were very firm and succulent. And her skin, like her complexion was unblemished and pale, even down to her cleanly shaven pussy.

They both made for the buffet for a drink and a nibble. Chelsea's eyes lit up as she spied a plate of six inch Frankfurter sausages. 'Oh look Mike,' she said in an enthusiastic manner, 'Gina has provided spare cocks in case we run out.'

She immediately picked one up and dipped it into the mayonnaise. Then seductively putting it into her mouth she started to suck the end. As she inserted it further into her mouth, with an evil twinkle in her eye, a line of mayo trickled down her chin and a small wave of the stuff flowed down the length of the sausage. The effect was awesome and Carl was immediately into action and a giant close up of Chelsea's sausage blow job filled the screen. From that moment on Carl never stopped filming and as more guests started to arrive, the pace of the action picked up. The carefully arranged script was abandoned and the inevitable orgy ensued.

Carl had taken Chelsea and an equally naked Mike over to one of the armchairs. Mike now had charge of the Frankfurter and as Chelsea sat on the edge of the chair, leaning backwards, she opened her legs. Mike knelt down and gently stroked her clitoris with the sausage. Chelsea purred her approval and gently slid her fingers down across her ample breasts and her tummy until they reached her pussy. She slowly and gracefully pulled her cunt lips apart to reveal the beautiful pink moist flesh inside. She moaned quietly as Mike slid the sausage inside her. He pushed it as far as it would go; just holding the end in his finger and thumb, then slid it in and out of her like a penis. She loved it and so did we, marvelling at the image on the big screen. Her appetite was incredible, as was Mike's. He put his head between her legs and took the end of the sausage in his mouth and pulled it slightly out of Chelsea's cunt. He bit the end off and ate it. Then he pulled a little more out and ate that and continued until he had finished the whole sausage.

'You've eaten my sausage,' she complained, 'now you've got to give me yours.'

Chelsea stood up and picked up a pouf which she placed in front of the armchair. She grabbed Mike's arms and bought him to his feet, her breasts tightening beautifully as she did so. She backed Mike up to the pouf and ordered him to sit. He did so and she pushed his shoulders back so he lay flat on the armchair, his hips supported by the pouf. Carl moved in for a close up of Mike's penis, it was indeed a sight to behold, a fact I could testify to as I had had it inside me on more than one occasion. Mike knew what was coming and he held his shaft upright from the base. It must have been a good nine inches of rock hard pulsating manhood. The veins stood out like whipcord and his huge end almost seemed to pulsate like a beacon in the night, bright purple with a clearly defined rim that any woman would love to have rippling against the sides of their cunt. But for the moment Chelsea was going to be that lucky woman. The room was silent, everyone's eyes on Chelsea and Mike and their image on the screen.

Chelsea moved forward, her eyes on Mike's pulsating shaft, she gracefully straddled him and as she stood there looking down on his manhood Mike seemed to whimper as he pointed his cock skyward ready to accept its destiny. She took his knob end and lowered herself onto it, pausing for a second to position it between her lips. Placing her hands on the arms of the chair she slowly lowered herself onto him. It was a wondrous sight to see her lips stretching as Mikes cock slid inside her cunt. They both moaned together as it slid ever further inside her. It seemed there was just an inch to go and Mike gripped her hips and forced her down on him. With a scream the last inch was inside her. She sat momentarily with Mike's full length inside her, and then she raised herself up, his shaft glistening with her love juice as her cunt lips sucked it. Almost at the top we could see the rim of his bulbous end and then she mercilessly dropped back onto him. With a moan his full length sank inside her. She continued this action a dozen or more times then she decided she wanted a different action, an action that would be more stimulating to her. Dropping down low onto him again, she leaned forward bracing herself against the arms of the chair. Then she gyrated her hips, sliding her clitoris against Mike's pelvis. His full length was inside her and she rubbed her clitty against him, his shaft must have shaken the inside of her cunt backwards and forwards. She was obviously in ecstasy as she thrust faster and faster and her huge tits banged up and down uncontrollably. It was an incredible sight, Chelsea was in a frenzy of pleasure, screaming and moaning and the image of that thrusting and her tits bouncing everywhere was unbelievable. She was thrusting her cunt hard onto his cock and grinding her clit into his pelvis. After a few moments more they seemed to explode into orgasm at the same time, Mike grasping her hips and forcing her down onto him even harder. Chelsea, with tears of pleasure rolling down her cheeks, screamed out in a fit of ecstasy as her knuckles turned white as she gripped the arms of the chair to force a little more pleasure out of her cunt. A cunt that was gripping and sucking the semen out of Mike's cock. The image of her cunt visibly gripping the base of his cock and the semen squelching out and mingling with his testicle was marvellous and the evening was just beginning. As they remained there, satisfied and getting their breath back a deserving round of applause filled the air.

The evening wore on and people of all ages, shapes and sizes, bonded by the common love of sexual pleasure, were having the time of their lives. People who had already performed were taking a welcome break while newcomers were always arriving and new blood would join the orgy.

Dear Joan was there and she had been set a challenge, after making a boast that she could take a hundred men in one night. Apparently there was quite a wager hanging on the outcome as a number of people had taken up the bet. The stipulation was that she had to have the semen of one hundred men, either on or inside her body by midnight. She certainly had her work cut out and in her favor there were certainly going to be more than one hundred men available throughout the evening and I had every confidence that Joan could take them all easily and more. Joan commandeered one of the bedrooms for her challenge and it was interesting to look in on her from time to time. She had apparently hedged her bet by arranging for the male members of a local supporters club to attend the evening solely for her pleasure and they arrived in a fifty seater bus so she was halfway home, if not all that dry.

An independent adjudicator was with her all the time to ensure accuracy and that her task was properly fulfilled. By ten o'clock she had almost secured her victory, the last four were with her and everyone was watching as if it was the final of a prestigious sporting event. Joan lay on the bed with her legs in the air supported by a very muscular looking blond

Adonis in his mid twenties. He had his shaft well inside her and was nearing his orgasm. He gave a shout of triumph as his semen shot inside her to mingle with all the other semen within her. This was quickly followed by another, who could have been a twin of the first and he shot his load deep into her mouth, which Joan devoured with great relish. Two others knelt either side of her on the bed and they jerked themselves off and came over her tits simultaneously. Joan was triumphant and her tits were covered completely in semen and as she lay exhausted on the bed as a river of semen oozed out of her glowing overworked cunt.

I went to get myself a drink and as I stood there a rich deep voice behind me said 'Hello Gina'.

I turned and gazed into the dark eyes of a hugely gorgeous man, a man who I recognised from the past.

'Remember me?'

I did indeed remember him and the memories immediately flooded back, it was Ted. Everyone has a great love in their life; Ted was that great love of my life. We had met when he was on leave from the army and I fell in love with him immediately. He had always been straight with me and told me that he had a fiancé in Germany, but I didn't care, I thought I could pull him away from her, but I was wrong, after two torrid weeks of brilliant sex, the army and his fiancé pulled him back to Germany. Time went on and he married his sweetheart and I married Carl. Things had moved on and his marriage, like so many, had floundered. He had heard about the movie through the friend of a mutual friend and when he had heard the name "Gina" mentioned, he had a gut feeling that it might be *his* Gina. His gut feeling was right.

'Ted.' I replied, after what must have seemed an interminable pause. 'How could I forget?'

We drank and talked about the old days and the future. I felt butterflies in my tummy and realised I still held the magic for Ted. Carl came over to get himself a drink. He was very pleased with his work so far but wanted something special and meaningful to finish the movie with. As he sipped his drink I saw a glint in his eye as he recognised the obvious rapport between Ted and me.

'Ah, the stars of the film.' He said with glee.

Without realising exactly how, we found ourselves in the main bedroom, our bedroom, the one room that had not been used by anyone else. The door was locked by Carl and the rest of the world seemed to disappear and fade into the mist of non existence. It was just Ted and me and the invisible Carl and his fly on the wall camera. I kicked off my shoes and we stood facing each other just staring into our eyes, it seemed as though we could communicate just by gazing. I felt my eyes filling up slightly as those memories of yesteryear came back to me. Ted stepped forward and took me in his strong arms and as his eyes gazed into mine our lips came closer and we kissed. He hugged me like the great bear of a man that he was and through his shirt I could feel his muscular body and the pounding of his heart. I also felt the unmistakable feeling of his erection pressing against my body. Ted was hot for it and he wasted no time. His kissing became very passionate and urgent, his hands under my vest and stroking my bare back, which soon came around and it quickly slid up my front until they clutched my breasts. He kissed and fondled me eagerly and in a flash he lifted my vest over my head and threw it across the room. Stepping backwards, his mouth was open as he took in the sight of my bare breasts. I shook them tantalisingly for him, making them shake and wobble. He gasped. I gave a little girlish giggle and shook them again for him. He undid his shirt, almost ripping it open, followed by his shoes, socks and trousers. He stood in just his shorts, a little damp patch just below the waistband from semen seeping from an obviously very erect and eager penis. Sliding down his shorts I gasped at the sight before me, it was the biggest cock I had seen that night. I had always remembered it been big, but it seemed to have grown over the years. Not only was it long, it was incredibly thick as well and it stood there gently bobbing and throbbing almost as if it was beckoning me forward. I moved to slide off my French knickers.

'No.' He barked. 'Leave them on. Get on the bed.'

I did as I was ordered. Mike lay next to me and kissed me gently. Once more I felt his hand travelling up my tummy to my breast and I sighed to myself as I felt his muscular hand gently cup it and caress it lovingly. He kissed my cheek and then my throat, slowly moving down my chest until he reached the breast he was still fondling. He kissed my nipple and flicked it with his tongue making it hugely erect. He played with me, gently nibbling my nipple with his lips and then his teeth. Sucking my nipples and opening his mouth wide and swallowing as much of my tit as he could get it into his mouth. As he devoured me I felt his searching fingers sliding down my belly. I knew where they were going and I yearned for him to reach his destination. His fingers slid over the delicate silky fabric of my knickers and his middle finger slid between my thighs. I opened my legs for him and his first finger pushed over the loose gusset of my knickers and I sighed as he ran his middle finger between my lips which were wet with anticipation. As his finger followed the line of my pussy lips I let out a little whimper as it gently stroked my clit. My whole body surged and came to life, feeling like a sexually starved nymphomaniac that needed to be satisfied. My whole being started to boil as he taunted and played with my womanhood. It was beautiful, too beautiful, never before had I been worked up to this point so quickly. I wanted Ted to fuck me, I wanted his huge cock inside me, stretching my cunt wide open and I wanted him now.

'Fuck me, fuck me now.' I begged.

Ted got between my legs; I opened them as wide and as high as I could, to present my cunt to its best advantage. I still had my knickers on but the gusset was well clear and I could feel my lips were open. Ted pointed his cock end between my eager cunt and slid inside me. It was wonderful, so thick and so hard; I could really feel it forcing its way inside me. I was incredibly juicy and it squelched as it slid inside. He had his arms extended either side of me and I felt the full splendour of his cock inside me. It felt brilliant as he slowly fucked me, his shaft almost coming out, I could feel the ridge of his giant knob end rub my clitoris. Then it sank deeply inside me again and once more his ridge rippling the inside of my cunt. He continued this steady pace for some time and I could have lain there for ever enjoying it.

'Do you want me to lick you?' He asked quietly and the thought of that thrilled me, I felt my cunt tingling again. I kept my position holding open my legs as Ted slid out of me kissing my breasts, my belly and finally his lips met my lips and his tongue immediately went to work on my clit. The pleasure was immediate and explosive, I knew I couldn't take much of this and Ted sensed my eagerness and licked me viciously. He gripped my silk covered buttocks in his hands almost lifting me up, his tongue licking my clit with such skill that I could feel an overwhelming surge of pleasure going through my body. I held my breath as it built up and then let out an enormous yell as the orgasm gripped me with cataclysmic force. I shook with the ultimate pleasure which just took over me. I screamed and cried and Ted licked harder and faster. Everything was there, that's the only way I can describe it. It went on forever, or so it seemed, then it slowly levelled out, but Ted kept licking. Then he stopped.

'Turn over and kneel on the edge of the bed.' He instructed in such a manner that I couldn't refuse.

Still gasping and weak with the exhaustion of pleasure I did as I was told. I kneeled and spread my legs. Ted stood behind me and I once more felt his knob end nuzzling against my cunt lips. He caressed my silk covered buttocks then took a firm grip on my hips and with an almighty thrust, his cock stabbed inside my cunt, going in up to the hilt. I let out another scream, this time it hurt me, but it was a strange hurt that was pleasurable, if that makes sense. Ted was incensed and he stabbed me wildly, each thrust seemingly going deeper than the last. I felt his fingers digging into my buttock flesh through my knickers. He was gasping with pleasure, he thrust harder and harder his huge ramrod of a cock pulverising my cunt. With one loud gasp I felt his hot semen shoot into my cunt, I could feel the rippling and throbbing of his big purple end as waves of his love juice filled my cunt and squelched out and flowed into my knickers. Ted, as exhausted as I was, pulled his shaft out of me and I felt his semen running down the inside of my thigh. I crawled onto the bed and collapsed. Ted flopped down beside me, his mighty cock now deflating and still oozing semen. A huge cheer went up from downstairs and it suddenly dawned on me that everyone had been watching.

'Absolutely wonderful. What a climax to the film.' Said Carl triumphantly with a big smile on his face. What a climax indeed.

THE END